Dancer

Killers Inc. #1

Charity Parkerson

Punk & Sissy Publications

Copyright

part in or encourage electronic piracy of copyrighted materials. Brief passages may be quoted for review purposes if credit is given to the copyright holder. Your support of the author's rights is appreciated. Any resemblances to person(s) living or dead, is completely co-incidental. All items contained within this novel are products of the author's imagination. AI was not used in any way to create this book. The author and publisher only support human artists.

—Warning: This book is intended for readers over the age of 18. Some of my books contain allusions to past abuse and trauma.

Contents

Introduction

AUSTEN KEEPS CRIMINALS ALIVE. Rain, being one of the world's deadliest assassins, doesn't scare him at all. He should.

As a private physician for the ultra-wealthy, Austen's entire business model rests on seeing nothing. After all, he keeps some of the biggest criminals on the west coast alive. That was how he ended up crossing paths with Rain. From first glance, he was stunned speechless by Rain's beauty. He can't stay away. That might be the thing that finally gets him killed.

As far as the world is concerned, Rain is a highly sought-after stage performer. Ballet has saved what little is left of his sanity. On the side, he just happens to kill people. When Austen starts showing up around every corner, Rain can't decide if he should kiss him or make him disappear. He's still trying to decide.

Dancer is the first book in Charity Parkerson's Killers Inc. series where hired assassins and their ilk find the love that finally saves them. These are best enjoyed when read in order.

Author Note

THIS SERIES IS ABOUT trained assassins. Assassins aren't born. They're forged. So, this series deals with several elements that shape hired killers. It has darker elements such as abuse, murder, and abduction.

Chapter One

BEFORE TWO MONTHS AGO, Austen had never been to the ballet. Now he made time for nearly every performance. Only if Rain Agafonov was a lead, of course. He rarely had much clue of what was going on. It still wasn't an art he understood. Austen could give two shits about anything except following Rain's every move with his gaze. He was tiny, beautiful, and pure grace. His every move screamed control. Blond hair and bright green eyes. He was fucking flawless. Rain also killed people. Austen shouldn't know that, but—in his profession—Austen had met a lot of killers. It wasn't his place to judge. Austen was a doctor. He kept people alive. Whatever they chose to do with those lives was on them. But Rain wasn't his patient, and Austen shouldn't know his secret. They had met very briefly through a mutual friend—one who was married to a criminal he knew well. That friend had later dropped the bomb. Austen was infatuated with a murderer. He didn't know how to stop.

Rain floated across the stage, looking as if he defied gravity. Austen sat in the front row and ate the man alive with his stare. For a moment, Austen thought Rain noticed him. The glance was over too quickly to hang on to it. When his phone buzzed with an incoming text, Austen knew it was all he would have for the night. Only emergency calls and texts could reach him after hours. He ground his back teeth and checked his phone. Sure enough, one of his longtime patients had od'd. They had been NARCANed back from the edge of death, but Austen would have to check on the situation. The rich were fucking exhausting. He didn't understand why they couldn't be content.

As he stood to quietly make his way toward the exit, he cast one last longing look Rain's way. For a second, he swore their gazes met. He knew it was likely wishful thinking. No doubt Rain couldn't see anyone's face clearly from the spotlights blasting him. But in an instant, Austen was back to that singular dance they'd shared. His friend, Kylo, had asked Austen to go with him on an errand. They had ended up at a small dance studio he had never noticed before. Inside, he found the most breathtaking tiny dancer he had ever seen. Rain had silently swept him into a dance. It had been an odd moment, but Austen had also been immediately ensnared. Longing struck like a bitch. Now here he was again, staring into those same eyes that kept bringing him back for more. Then Rain looked away, setting him free. Disappointment sat on his chest as he headed for the door. Some things weren't meant to be. Austen understood this was one of those things. To him, Rain was a case of limerence. He was stuck somewhere between the obsession and frustration stages. Austen didn't know how to move on to the resolution stage. Maybe he never would. He didn't know how to let go.

Somehow, Austen made it through checking on his patient. No one understood how tired he was. He had been going all hours of the day for a while now. While driving home, he searched his mind for ways to slow down. It was a familiar discussion with himself. Austen couldn't exactly hire help. His patients ranged from weapons dealers to drug lords and everything in between. Austen had patched up more bullet and stab wounds than he cared to recall. He did so with his mouth shut and got paid more than any other doctor could dream. There were patients he saw who weren't criminals. Athletes and such. Maybe he could shift those patients to a new doctor. The problem with that was they might still stumble upon something they shouldn't. He could close his practice completely and retire, but he wasn't sure if that would get him killed. Austen's mind stayed locked on the issue as he went through his nightly routine. Maybe if he went to bed right now, he could grab a few more hours of sleep than usual. Austen's shoulders fell. Who was he kidding? His dad had always told him nothing good happened after midnight. He'd been right. Most of the worst calls came in the middle of the night. He stared at his reflection. In only pajama pants, he studied himself. When had he gotten so old? One day, he had been a college football star, riding his best years through a scholarship and fighting his way toward this future. Now, there were wrinkles at the corners of his eyes and some gray threading his blond hair. He imagined he looked better than most people his age. That wasn't him being vain. He could afford to stay looking good. Soon, though, even that wouldn't help him, and he would still be alone.

Austen angrily turned off the light. His mind drifted to Rain again. No doubt Rain was too young for him. But if Austen had time to pursue him the way he wanted, maybe he would actually have a shot. He'd never know.

An image of Rain filled his head. He remembered every detail of the intense way Rain had stared at him with those light eyes. Austen's cock stirred. He could already picture those eyes turned up at him while Rain got on his knees. A shaky breath escaped him. He stared into the dark and fought the urge to shove his hand in his pants. Austen was tired of stroking himself to only the dream of Rain. He was tired of being alone.

The slightest sixth sense of being watched overcame him. An odd glow of light reflected from the wall where Austen's gaze had been locked. It moved slightly. In a flash, Austen rolled. A black-clad figure stood over him. The guy bolted the second he was spotted. Austen snatched his gun from the night-stand and went after him. He knew the house better than any intruder. Austen cut through the dining room and beat him to the door. The guy froze. He wore one of those electronic masks. The one that used LED lights to transform the face. The face looked shocked.

"Stay where you are."

The guy took a step back.

Austen snagged him before he got away. He was tiny and light as a feather. Austen wondered if it was a teenager. He didn't want to shoot a kid. The moment Austen held him, he went still. The eyes on the mask turned to pink hearts, confusing the fuck out of Austen. In his moment of surprise, the guy slipped from his arms. Austen tried again to grab him. The guy pulled some acrobatic move, completely dodging Austen. He tried several times to catch him, but it was as if he was made of rubber or some shit. Austen had never seen anyone bend and twist so quickly and effortlessly. Then his feet were swept from beneath him. He hit the floor. While it knocked the wind from him, he had somehow landed on a mountain of pillows that should have been on the couch. He stared at the ceiling. Austen knew without looking his nighttime visitor was gone.

He rolled to his knees. Forty-three was too old to lose a fight. He pushed to his feet. The front door stood open.

Austen looked out, even though he knew he wouldn't find anything. The security lights flared to life, making Austen wonder how in the hell the guy had gone out this way and not done the same. A single rose in a crystal vase waited for him. Austen blinked. He moved slowly. Even Austen didn't know why he was hesitant to grab it. Once he had it in his hand, his confusion shot to the heavens. It was real crystal. Austen had a lot of money and liked nice things. It was a very expensive vase. He eyed the front lawn and driveway. His gaze slid up and down the street. Nothing stirred. He had no clue what had just happened, but he prayed a patient hadn't decided he knew too much. His gaze dropped to the rose. Maybe it was a warning of his upcoming death. What was he supposed to do now?

Dr. Austen Flowers truly was beautiful. From Rain's experience, there were a lot of gorgeous men in the world. No one had ever struck him as so flawless. It was the way Austen looked at him. His stare always held more than adoration. Pure obsession poured from Austen's eyes each time their gazes met. Rain just wanted to see him. Look at him. He hadn't expected to get caught. No one had ever snatched him from his feet before he could get away like that. Austen had been fast as fuck when he realized he wasn't alone. Of course, once he had been caught, Rain's training had kicked in. He had known he would have to take Austen down to get away. That was why he had grabbed a cushion each time he dodged Austen. He needed Austen to have a softer fall. Still, he felt guilty. He never meant to scare him. Rain had only meant to drop off a gift. But longing had gotten the best of him and Rain had to see him. He wanted to kick himself for his carelessness.

"Where have you been? You sure as fuck had better not been doing a job without us again."

Edge was always so fucking quiet. Rain hadn't noticed him sitting in the corner chair, reading, as he came through the door. "Hey. I didn't. I just needed a break."

Edge's light-brown gaze dropped to the mask Rain held. "A break."

Rain refused to acknowledge his gear. "Yes."

A loud sigh cut through the air as Edge snapped his book closed. "Off-the-books jobs are becoming a bad habit of yours."

While Rain hated to answer to anyone, he understood Edge's concern. Every-thing each did affected the others. They couldn't have unexpected dead bodies leading to them. That hadn't stopped Rain from making a problem disappear for his friend Kylo. He got why Edge worried. "I promise it was nothing like that." He held Edge's stare so he could see his honesty.

Edge gave him a sharp nod and re-opened his book. "I hear your perfor-mance was perfect tonight."

"Isn't it always?"

The corner of Edge's mouth lifted, taking some of his natural darkness away.

Assuming they were through, Rain jogged up the steps and fled to the safety of his bedroom. He tossed his stuff on the chair next to the bed and stripped. Rain had rushed straight from the theater to Austen's place after the performance. He hadn't had a chance to shower. Plus, he just slept better after steaming himself clean. Rain's mind was never at peace. He needed all the help he could get.

Standing under the deluge of hot water, Austen played through Rain's mind. He had been watching Austen for a while. The night he had unexpectedly shown up at Rain's dance studio, Rain had been in a bad place mentally. His friend Kylo had appeared with Austen in tow. Rain's gaze had kept sliding toward the man. While their meeting had been short, Rain's mood had lifted just being in his company. Still, Rain had let the moment go. Then Austen had turned up in the front row of his next performance. At first, all of Rain's alarms had blared. In his business, there was no such thing as coincidences. The moment he had been freed from the theater, Rain had done what he did best: hunted.

For a while, Rain thought Austen knew Rain was onto him and simply pretended to live a boring yet exhausting life. Finally, Rain had been forced to accept Austen came to his shows for him. He knew it was for him. Austen's eyes never left him. He did something to Rain's chest. Rain's body stirred as he pictured those blue eyes and the way he stared at Rain with longing—like a drowning man. Crazy could be hot as hell. Rain slid his hand down his stomach. He ached to have that insanity unleashed on him. Rain bet good money Austen was an intense lover. He needed that. Rain dragged out the anticipation. He lightly stroked himself before he tightened his grip. Behind his closed eyelids, Rain saw Austen and the things Rain could do to his body. He understood Austen was older than him, but the numbers didn't matter. Rain wanted that experience. He felt in his bones Austen would fuck him hard. Rain practically felt Austen pounding him. He stroked fast. His hips rolled, riding his palm. An orgasm struck hard and fast as he pictured Austen whispering his name. Rain dropped his gaze and stared down the line of his body. Emptiness washed over him. He was still alone. That was safer for both of them. He should let Austen stay a fantasy—the way he did every man that caught his eye.

His hands rose. Rain stared at his palms. His vision blurred. Austen's hands saved lives. Rain's took life. Sometimes his mind was a terrifying place. He should forget Austen. Rain wasn't good. A howling wind whipped through him where Rain's conscience should be. He couldn't change. He had to let this go.

Chapter Two

THE LIGHTS SEEMED ULTRA hot tonight. His legs were extra tired. Austen sat in the front row again and Rain kept glancing his way. He wondered how much longer Austen would stalk him before giving up. The idea of not seeing his face in the crowd hurt Rain's chest. He wanted to talk to him. Just once. Rain needed to know if whatever drove him to be this obsessed existed or if he had built Austen up inside his mind to be someone he wasn't.

Picking the least disruptive moment, Rain twirled off stage and nodded for his backup to take over. They were all professionals who trained tirelessly. He didn't doubt the man's ability to step in seamlessly.

Rain grabbed the closest stagehand. "There's a guy. Front row. Third seat from the left. He's my doctor. Please grab him and bring him back here."

Sven's gaze moved over Rain's features. "Are you okay?"

"Not really."

That was enough to send Sven scurrying. Rain never missed even part of a performance. He danced through every illness and injury. Truthfully, this felt a lot like swallowing his pride, but an excuse was an excuse.

Rain dramatically limped his way to the dressing room and worked to unwind his ballet shoes. His feet looked awful. That was part of the game. Tonight, his foot looked especially bad.

"He's right through here."

Austen appeared like a man on a white horse, his face etched with concern, while his gaze locked on Rain and didn't budge. He was beautiful. "Are you okay? That guy said you needed a doctor."

Rain tried not to purr like a contented cat. Austen sounded like he really cared. It was no wonder he had such an extensive and exclusive list of patients.

"Sorry to pull you from the show. I know you haven't gotten to see a full one yet." Austen always left partway through.

The blush that tinted Austen's cheeks nearly made Rain moan. Damn. He had never wanted anyone like this. "Don't worry about it. I'm only here for you." He cleared his throat, sounding adorably nervous. "I don't know why I said that. Tell me what's wrong." His confidence visibly returned at the demand. Taking care of people was obviously his comfort zone.

Rain glanced toward his foot. "As much as I hate to scar you with the horrors of ballet feet, I think I've injured myself. Kylo tells me you're an amazing doctor. I'm sure there's some procedure I'm not following here to hire your services, but I don't want to go to the emergency room."

Austen's concern visibly deepened. A line appeared between his brows. He dropped to his knees like he didn't currently wear a five-figure tux. Austen gently brought Rain's foot to his knee.

Rain studied him while Austen inspected his foot. He was the typical California pretty, but he had something no one else did. It was a kindness that softened him. Rain had nothing soft in his life.

"I'm surprised you could see me with those lights in your face."

Ah. Austen thought his stalking had gone unnoticed. "You get used to it."

Austen nodded. "Without X-rays, I can't give you a definitive diagnosis, but this looks like a dancer's fracture."

Rain had already known that. He had been dancing on it since the show's run began. The end of production was around the corner. He could get it treated then. Rain just needed the excuse to talk to Austen without making it weird.

"I was afraid of that." He sighed dramatically. "Send me your bill and I will get it taken care of after the show ends for the season."

Austen's chin shot up. His gaze latched on to Rain's face. "If you wait, you're risking internal damage and permanent deformity that could lead to you never dancing or walking properly again. Not to mention the constant pain."

He was so passionate. Rain couldn't look away. "What would you have me do?"

Austen chewed his bottom lip. It was obvious he understood they discussed Rain's career. While it wasn't his breadwinner, it was his passion. Finally, he sighed. "Stay off it the rest of the night. Let me take you home, put some ice on it, and ensure you don't put an ounce of pressure on it. Tomorrow, I'll do your X-rays and we'll go from there."

Rain's smile had appeared at the mention of taking him home and hadn't dimmed. "So you wish to take me home?" His Russian accent came out thick in his humor and desire. It was out of his control.

Austen's gaze moved over his face. "Yes."

Damnit. He still wasn't sure how Austen meant the exchange. Austen was too professional. Too hard to read. It was possible he didn't realize Rain flirted. He released another loud, dramatic sigh. "If you must. I'm at your mercy."

To his surprise, Austen stood and swept Rain into his arms, as if he weighed nothing. "You can count on me to make sure your car makes it home. I'll take care of everything."

Rain wrapped his arms around Austen's neck and settled in for the ride. He was invested as hell. When he had impulsively made this decision, this was the last thing he expected. He wasn't disappointed. "I get the impression you're a very steady and reliable man."

A wry smile touched Austen's lips that sent butterflies stirring in his stomach. "Although I'm sure you meant that as a compliment, I feel old now. Thanks for that."

Rain threw his head back and laughed. It wasn't what Austen said. It was his tone. He obviously had a dry wit. "I assure you. You don't feel old at all to me."

Sven rushed to open the door, leading them to the parking lot from a side entrance. As much as Rain recognized he got what he craved by being in Austen's arms, he didn't want to be seen getting carried out injured. This was a cut-throat business. He had to stay on top.

Austen easily carried Rain through the large parking lot without getting winded. The lights flashed on the man's BMW SUV as they neared. Rain grabbed the handle on the passenger side, doing his part. Together, they got Rain strapped in without him putting any pressure on his foot—just as Austen promised.

As Austen circled the vehicle, Rain took a few breaths. This was dumb. Edge would fucking die when Rain showed up with Austen. He would be exposing their home, but Rain wasn't an idiot. After the first time they met, Rain had investigated every inch of Austen's life. He truly appeared to be merely an overworked doctor. For one night, Rain wanted something for himself. He had never been shy about taking it.

With address in hand, they were on the road. Austen could barely breathe. He couldn't believe this was happening. Rain was in his car. They were together.

Technically, Rain was his patient, but still. They were alone. Horror washed through him each time he recalled that Rain knew he had been to every performance. He looked like a stalker. Rain didn't seem upset, though. Damn. They were really together. Even the silence between them was nice.

"So, you're friends with Kylo."

A laugh burst from Austen. "Sorry. It seems so strange. Before tonight, we met that one time when I was with Kylo and said less than a handful of words to each other. Yet I'm just sitting here in silence, like you've known me forever. I didn't mean to make you uncomfortable. Yes, I'm friends with Kylo. I'm also his doctor, which came first. That's probably not ethical, but I work for myself, so whatever."

"I'm glad you feel that way. It's odd to have such a personal relationship with a doctor yet be divided by ethics. Also, I'm not uncomfortable. It's impossible to rattle me. I've spent my entire life under the harshest of scrutiny on stage. Kylo tells me you saved his life."

Austen supposed that was true. Kylo had been stabbed during a mugging outside a grocery store. His now husband, Beau, had called Austen. Since Beau was the biggest weapons dealer on the west coast and a major source of income for Austen, Austen had immediately dropped everything. Still... "I'm fairly certain, if I hadn't helped, Kylo would've just hiked up his shirt and stitched himself closed." Austen couldn't help the humor in his voice. "He's easily the strongest and most stubborn person I've ever met."

"You like him."

The comment confused Austen. He had just said they were friends. "Of course, he's my friend."

"No." The denial was quiet—like Rain studied him and assured himself of whatever answer he had found. "You like him in a sexual way."

Austen nearly steered off the road in his surprise.

Rain didn't stop there. "That's to be expected, honestly. Not only is he extremely beautiful, as you said, he's strong. But he's also gentle and a nice place to land in a cold world."

As Austen listened to the variance in Rain's voice, the truth struck him. It was a bit devastating. "You love him."

A soft chuckle rumbled from the passenger seat. "I do. We've spent many nights together, working and talking. He's quite amazing in countless ways. But I don't think I love him in the way you meant. He is family to me. I learned quickly over the years to appreciate the people who make me a part of their lives like I'm just as good as blood. He's always cared for me. I'd kill for him." A soft chuckle followed the words, and a chill ran down Austen's spine. He wondered how fucked up in the head he was. The night he had gone with Kylo to see Rain, Kylo had gone there for exactly that reason. He had asked Rain to kill someone. Austen hadn't been horrified then, and he wasn't now. Maybe he was desensitized after all these years of stitching up criminals. Whatever the reason, not only was he completely un-

bothered, he found it hot that such a perfect porcelain doll was also what Kylo
described as the world's deadliest assassin. He didn't know how safe he was
with that info.

Austen chose to be open about himself
and hope that helped ease the way to
freely speaking in the future. "As to
your accusation, when I first met Kylo,
yes. He impressed the hell out of me
with everything about himself, and I
wanted more. Then he fell for Beau,
and I lost my chance. That's how my
life goes, though. My job is so busy,
it wrecks everything. Like seeing your
performance," he added with a laugh.
"I've been called away every single time
I try to see it." Austen started to add he
supposed with Rain hurt, he wouldn't
get to see it now. Another thought hit,
redirecting him. He had been so thrilled

to have Rain with him, he had pushed aside the reason he was there. "Are you in pain? I should've asked that first. We can swing by my place and go ahead and get those X-rays. While there, I can get you some pain meds."

Rain didn't respond right away. Finally, he sighed. "As much as I'd love to say yes and keep you for myself longer, I don't like the idea of pain medicine. It could make me slow and I—" Rain stopped dead, as if almost saying too much. He started again. "I don't take medicine like that unless absolutely necessary."

It could get him killed. That was what Rain couldn't say, and Austen got it. He spent his days around dangerous people. In fact, he worried that was exactly why his home had been broken into. He, too, spent his time with criminals.

Austen was way more concerned about it than he cared to admit. In fact, he seriously considered taking the matter to Kylo's husband. He knew Beau would know how to handle this.

"I've made you quiet. It wasn't an insult against your profession. I know you're only hoping to help."

Austen flashed a smile Rain's way. "No. It's not you. I'm just tired, I suppose." Thankfully, Rain's house came into view, saving him from saying anything else. In fact, his entire brain wiped. The place was massive. He supposed murder paid well. The dwelling was only about half the size of Beau Bosi's residence. Once again, proving crime paid, Beau's place was a compound, spreading out over acres. He couldn't say that about Rain's house. It looked like a home. Still, a nervous laugh escaped him at the luxury of it. "Your skills are showing. This is a beautiful place."

Musical laughter caressed his ears. "Don't be too impressed. I don't live alone. When I moved to this country, my brothers came with me. We share a home."

Austen nodded. He didn't feel better. The house was still enormous. Unless Rain had twenty brothers, it seemed excessive.

Rain pointed toward an almost hidden secondary driveway next to the five-car garage. "Follow that. It will end near a back way inside. We can avoid the family. They can be overwhelming."

At least there was that. He didn't relish meeting any overprotective brothers. No matter how deadly Rain might be, he was also delicate-looking. No doubt his family watched over him like pit bulls. Austen parked where told before he had Rain in his arms again. He knew he could have helped him limp, but Rain was tiny, and Austen wanted to hold him.

Austen stood at the back door while Rain used his thumbprint to unlock the door. After Rain pushed the door open, Austen carried him inside and kicked the door closed behind him.

Rain pointed at a staircase that looked like one used for employees, so they weren't seen. "I'm upstairs. If you want, I can hop."

A wicked-sounding chuckle slipped from Austen before he could stop it. He headed up the stairs. "I've got you." Austen felt Rain's stare, but he kept his gaze focused ahead. He couldn't see Rain's reaction to that laugh. It had sounded like all the naughty things Austen wanted to do to Rain. He had to reel it back in.

At the top of the steps, Rain pointed left and then right when he reached a bedroom. It was oddly... lacking in comfort. Austen didn't know how to explain the empty plainness. Everything was very monochromatic. Austen carried him to the bed and reluctantly got him settled.

"Tell me what else you need before..." Austen's gaze locked on the chair near the bed. A familiar black jacket and an electronic mask stared back at him. For a second, he spaced out. He focused on Rain.

Rain chewed the side of his nail, looking nervous. That said everything Austen needed to know.

The air left Austen's lungs. Rain killed people. He had been in Austen's house. Austen would wonder if this was a ruse, but the injury was real. Still, Rain could have used the injury to lure Austen into a trap.

"I just wanted to see you," Rain said, finally breaking the silence.

"You just wanted..." The rage hit without warning. Why couldn't he just meet someone nice? "Why didn't you ring the doorbell? I swear to God. All men are the same. Did it ever occur to you to try not manipulating me? I would've been fucking thrilled to see you. Is this all a ploy?" Austen swiped his hand through the air. He was beyond upset. "Don't answer that. It doesn't matter." Austen headed for the door. He was done. Rain had left him fearing for his life. He knew Rain didn't understand. Austen lived in a precarious place. He always expected exactly what happened and Rain had only wanted to see him? Fuck. He had spent the whole day feeling sick.

"Who the fuck are you?"

Austen drew up short at the bottom of the steps. A huge, red-haired guy with a spoon and a full jar of peanut butter waited for Austen to gather his wits. If this was a brother, he looked nothing like Rain.

"Dr. Flowers." He motioned over his shoulder. "Rain was injured during tonight's performance. I brought him home."

The guy's brows drew together, making his dark green stare look even more deadly.

A dark-haired guy appeared from a side door. He pulled up short. "Who are you?"

The red-haired one motioned his way with the spoon. "This one claims Rain is hurt."

Dark brows shot upward. Light brown eyes latched on to him. "Is that so?"

Austen's hands lifted and fell. "I suspect a dancer's fracture, but I won't know for sure until he's been X-rayed." So

Austen assumed he would never know. He didn't intend to see Rain again.

Both men pushed past him and headed for the stairs. "Rain's foot would fall off before he admitted to hurting."

That didn't surprise Austen. Since it seemed his job was done, he let himself out. Rain had family to care for him. He was free of any obligation to a liar. Austen ignored the tiny voice in the back of his head that whispered Rain hadn't lied. In fact, he hadn't even tried to deny being the person who broke into his home. There was also another voice reminding Austen he had been stalking Rain too. But Austen hadn't hidden, for fuck's sake. He hadn't intentionally scared Rain or put Rain on his ass. The memory of those LED lights turning to hearts sneaked in, making Austen's chest hurt. He had truly enjoyed the idea of Rain. It seemed he had a bigger problem with insanity than he thought. He didn't want to be on the receiving end.

Chapter Three

AUSTEN MADE HIS WAY from store to store. Rain followed at a distance. He liked watching Austen walk, even though he looked upset today. That was Rain's fault. Rain was a psychopath first and everything else second. He didn't know how to pursue someone when he didn't plan to kill them. Rain had likely blown his chance. He understood he looked as crazy as he was. His current actions didn't help, but he couldn't stop.

As Austen headed to his SUV with shopping bags in hand, Rain kept time with his steps. It was almost a dance of sorts. Without thinking, Rain twirled and created his own routine with only Austen's pace. He spun again and came face to face with an amused-looking Austen. It seemed his inability to be normal busted his stalking.

"So you really were just using that injury to see me."

It wasn't a question, but Rain went onto the toes of that foot and twirled. He stopped chest to chest with Austen. "I actually fractured it at the beginning of the show's run. It can wait until the show ends."

Austen shook his head. "Did you and Kylo sign some sort of pact to be the world's worst patients? Just stubborn."

Rain shrugged. "I don't know about Kylo, but I'm good. This is nothing. You ran away last night before I got the chance to explain."

Austen's chest expanded as if he took a deep breath for patience. "Okay."

Rain wouldn't miss his chance twice. He struck without warning. Rain used his quick agility against Austen, climbing Austen's body and claiming his mouth. Rain didn't hold back. He had only intended to steal a small kiss and then beg forgiveness. Except Austen turned so fucking passionate that Rain couldn't pull away. Austen's bags dropped to the ground. He gripped Rain's nape and controlled him. Austen kissed Rain like the most desperate of whores. Adrenaline and lust made it hard for Rain to breathe. By the time he pulled away, they simply stared at each other and struggled to catch their breath. Rain held two handfuls of Austen's shirt and he couldn't let go. Austen's gaze dropped to Rain's mouth again and Rain feared for the last dregs of his sanity.

"I accept your explanation."

A bark of laughter burst from Rain. Damn. He really liked Austen. He still felt moved to be honest. "I'm a little psycho."

"That's okay." Austen recaptured his mouth, taking back their hot kiss and burning Rain to the ground. Finally, Austen pulled away, but he didn't release Rain. "Come home with me."

"Okay."

"I want to X-ray that foot."

Rain chuckled. Of course he did. Austen was the good guy. Rain wasn't. He would go home with Austen. That got them one step closer to bed. "Still okay."

A smile exploded across Austen's face. "Do you want to ride with me or follow?"

"I'll follow." He didn't want Austen to change his mind at some point and toss him out without a ride. That kiss might have addled his brain for now, but that fog wouldn't last forever.

"That's probably for the best. I never know when I'll get called in."

Disappointment washed over Rain. He knew there was a high chance that could happen. Still, he tried not to show it. "It's your job."

A sweet smile touched Austen's lips. "If I can avoid it, I won't go. I have nurses

I can send." Before he had time to respond, Austen stole another quick kiss. "I'll see you there."

Rain nodded and took a step back. "Okay." He forced himself to walk away and get in his car. As he buckled in, he noticed Austen still standing in the same spot, watching. Finally, he shook his head and walked off. A laugh burst from Rain. He knew he had Austen fucked up. To be fair, he was pretty messed up over this too. It wasn't good for him to want anyone. He could put Austen in danger. For once, Rain couldn't stop himself from reaching out for someone. He desperately wanted this, and he hadn't lied. Rain was psycho. He would do what he wanted with zero good sense no matter what, so it was best to start this way. God help him when his family caught wind of this. They would put Austen through the wringer.

What was he doing? Without Rain there to scatter his thoughts, Austen questioned his sanity. The guy had broken into his house just to see him. Butterflies stirred in Austen's gut at the thought. That was kind of hot. Now that he had gotten past the shock of realizing it was Rain that night, and not a patient out to silence him, Austen was a little moved. After all, technically, he had been kind of, sort of stalking Rain too. This was the first time anyone had done anything crazy for him. It was kind of flattering. Who was he kidding? Austen was blown away. He was likely at least fifteen years older than Rain, and Rain was desirable in every way. He wanted this way more than he wanted to admit. Austen was almost scared of himself.

The drive home took too long, even though it was the usual fifteen minutes. He kept checking his rearview mirror, ensuring Rain hadn't disappeared. When they both climbed from their vehicles again, Austen couldn't stop the huge grin that stretched his lips. Rain was so fucking beautiful. His every move was so light and bouncy, as if he danced inside his head.

"Let's get that X-ray."

Rain rolled his eyes, but he grabbed Austen's bags for him, took his arm, and held on. "Let's go. You won't be able to focus on anything else until you've had your way."

Damn. He really wanted to have his way with Rain. Austen was better than this. Rain deserved to be pampered and respected. Austen wanted to give him all the attention. Inside, he led Rain to his home office and dragged out the portable X-ray machine. Rain quietly cooperated with every instruction.

He found the lead drape. "Any chance you might be pregnant?" He was so dumb and cheesy. Austen heard himself.

Rain didn't call him on it. He leaned into it. "Are you volunteering to be the daddy?" There was so much sexy teasing in Rain's voice that they froze and held each other's stare.

"Absolutely." Even Austen heard how serious he sounded. He sure as hell wouldn't say no.

"Then we should definitely move this along."

With a nod, Austen dragged a lead barrier into place and took the pictures he needed. He tried hard to stay in doctor mode as he studied the images. Austen didn't like what he saw. He couldn't believe Rain was walking around without even a limp, never mind dancing a full performance every night.

"You have a very serious look about you."

Austen kept his gaze locked on the images. "I think it's very likely you need surgery." He focused on Rain. "If you don't take care of this, it'll be career-ending." Austen hated delivering that news, but Rain was destroying his bone structure.

"If I stop to have surgery before the end of the run, I'll be ending my career. I'm already older than any other dancer on that stage. The moment I step aside, I'm done."

It was the first time he had seen Rain completely serious and without a hint of wickedness. He was captivated.

"This is my dream. I know it isn't forever, but it's not over yet. I'm not ready for it to be over yet."

Austen had never seen such powerful passion in anyone's eyes. Rain would get back on that stage even if every bone in his body was broken. Austen puffed out his cheeks and blew out a slow breath.

He calculated how long there was left in the run and weighed that number against the risks. The doctor in him couldn't let this go completely.

"The second that final show ends, let me do the surgery. Not only am I the best, but I can also take care of you while you heal. I can make sure you're back dancing in perfect condition for your next role."

To his surprise, Rain didn't hesitate. "Deal."

Rain glanced around, as if suddenly uncomfortable. "So what do we do now?"

"I want to know you."

Rain's eyes danced with laughter as he focused on Austen again. "You really don't."

Austen kept his expression as serious as he was. "No. I really do." He rolled his chair to where Rain sat with his legs dangling over the edge of his patient table. Austen moved until he sat between Rain's feet. He ran his hands up Rain's thighs. Since Rain already knew Austen had been coming to every show and they had equally made fools of themselves, he chose honesty. "I don't know what happened the night we met. It was a few short minutes out of time, but it was enough. You say you're psycho. Maybe I'm crazy too because I haven't thought about anyone else since that night." There was something needy in Rain's eyes that kept Austen's lips moving. "I don't know why I can't stay away from you, but I want to find out." His biggest insecurity washed over him and fell from his lips. "No one chooses me. I'm overworked and exhausted. I never get to pursue anyone with the focus they deserve. More likely than not, you'll be done with me pretty damn fast. But I want to try. I need to know why I can't stop thinking about you."

Rain slipped from the table and straddled Austen's lap.

Austen held him close, keeping him from landing on the floor. Rain weighed nothing. Austen kind of enjoyed manhandling him.

Light green eyes focused on him with a burning intensity. "Once you know me, you'll hate me. I like this version you have in your head and I'm terrible enough to use it to my advantage." He skimmed his lips across Austen's for a moment before diving deeper. Just as Austen knew it would, their kiss turned hot in a flash. Austen kneaded Rain's ass and rocked Rain's lower body against him. He kept trying to stop, but each time, he would immediately start again. His neglected body was engulfed in white-hot desire. Austen snapped. He stood with Rain's ass still filling his hands. Rain wrapped his legs around Austen as Austen headed for his bedroom. He knew he should slow down, but he also knew he likely wouldn't get this chance again. Rain didn't sound like he wanted Austen in his life for real. Austen couldn't let him get away without tasting him.

The second he had Rain on his back, he kissed a path down Rain's body. He wanted this so goddamn badly. Weeks of watching Rain and dreaming were crushing his chest now. Austen had never been so close to touching a real-life fantasy. He popped the button on Rain's jeans. His emergency phone rang. Austen froze. He squeezed his eyes shut and fought the swelling in his throat. Why wasn't he allowed this one thing?

Rain cupped his jaw and forced Austen to meet his stare. He knew there was no hiding the devastation in his eyes. Rain's gaze moved over his face. "Go. I'm not going anywhere. In fact, I'll stick a pillow under my foot and watch TV while you're gone. I'll be the good little patient." A wicked smile touched his lips. "Then I'll be very bad when you get back."

Austen was beyond enraptured with Rain. "I really want this thing with you, and I don't mean sex."

Rain's thumb brushed Austen's bottom lip. "I'm not going anywhere," he repeated quietly.

Something new stirred inside Austen. He would hurry home, and he would give this his all. Rain planned to meet him more than halfway. It felt like a miracle.

Chapter Four

DESPITE HIS BEST EFFORTS, Austen's bitterness grew on the way to Beau Bosi's home. Beau was a deadly weapons dealer and Austen had done a lot of patching up around his place. He had hoped when Beau had married the love of his life, he would stop needing Austen quite so much. At least this time, it was a sick guard who was apparently at death's door from some mystery ailment and not a gunshot wound. Still, Austen just wanted to be home in bed with Rain. Damn, he really hoped Rain truly meant to wait. He needed this in his life.

Austen pulled into the circular drive-way of Beau's compound and parked at the bottom of the front steps. The front door flew open as soon as Austen jogged up the stairs.

A frazzled-looking Henry waited for him. That turned Austen's blood cold. Beau's longtime guard was as ruthless as they came. Austen had never seen him out of sorts. His light brown eyes were filled with terror.

He waved Austen inside. "Come on. He's upstairs."

"Tell me what's going on. What are the symptoms?"

Henry spoke as he jogged up the steps. "I found him on the bathroom floor this morning when he didn't show up for his shift. He was barely lucid and apparently had passed out after puking." He threw the door open to one of the rooms. Another of Beau's guards, Mickey, was curled into a ball on the bed naked. His skin was bright red and sweat covered his body. A bad and irritating feeling washed over Austen. Beau and Kylo sat next to the bed.

Austen pulled a mask from his pocket and put it on. He touched Mickey's leg as he moved closer. His skin was on fire, and he shook. "Hey there, Mickey. It's Austen. Can you tell me what's going on?"

Green eyes focused on him. His blond hair was plastered to his face. "It's a damn virus or the flu or something. I told them not to call you. This'll pass."

Austen had to agree. It was flu season and had been going around hard. That was exactly why he had a few tests in his bag. "Let's do a quick flu test, then we'll work on this fever." Austen spoke as he went through the motions. "Have you kept any liquids down?"

"I've been forcing water in him," Kylo said, looking scared.

He was such a sweet guy. His big blue eyes and blond hair made him look innocent as hell. Today, he had bows in his hair and wore one-piece pajamas with unicorns all over it.

Austen nodded and set the test aside to do its thing. "Let's get some fever reducer in you." He pinched a small piece of skin on Mickey's hand, checking for dehydration. Austen's aggravation grew when he looked fine. He wasn't unsympathetic. This just wasn't an emergency. They had called his emergency line for a virus. It was obvious they didn't respect his time. They thought they owned him. His bedside manner turned shittier and shittier by the second until he was simply going through the motions. The flu test came back positive.

Austen whipped out his prescription pad with more force than necessary. "I'm writing a prescription for an antiviral medication." He scratched out the script. "I'll also go ahead and write one for each of you to start, so you hopefully won't catch this." Even his handwriting looked angry.

He ripped off the papers and put them on the bedside table. "There. I hope you feel better soon."

Without as much as a goodbye, Austen headed for the door.

Beau was in his path before he made it five steps. "What's wrong?"

Austen's eye twitched. "It's nothing." He stepped around Beau, and Beau stepped back into his path. This time, Beau looked like the crime boss he was. "No, really. What's wrong with you?" His hard tone said Austen wouldn't be leaving there without answering.

Austen opened his mouth to give a half-ass excuse so he could get out of there. That wasn't what happened. "None of you respect my goddamn time. Emergency phones are for emergencies. Not the flu." He looked over his shoulder at Mickey. "Not that I don't care."

Mickey nodded. "I know." His voice sounded scratchy.

Austen focused on Beau again. His anger hadn't lessened. "I'll always show up when you need me, but I have a life too. I let you spend time with your family. Your man. Why can't you call the non-emergency line when I'm off so I can write scripts from home, and I can spend some time with my fucking man? Goddamn." He recognized he practically yelled, but Austen was so over it. He was literally one wrong word away from walking away from this career and letting the chips fall. Austen was so fed up.

Beau's expression was blank. His dark eyes held the same glint of danger they always did. Beau possessed something absolutely terrifying that couldn't be described. It was felt.

Kylo appeared at Beau's side. "I'm sorry we called you away from Rain. Why didn't you tell us you need help? Surely we can figure out something so you're not overworked."

Austen was so taken aback by Kylo knowing he meant Rain that his brain froze.

Beau's obviously didn't. "You're dating Rain? Rain Agafonov? The assassin?"

Austen pinched the spot between his eyes. "That's the one."

Beau nodded, looking entirely too thoughtful. "I'll put the word out tomorrow. With my connections, it won't take long to find a couple of passable physicians who can help carry the load in this town. You should've said something."

The offer felt suspect. Beau didn't do nice things for people. That didn't mean Austen wouldn't accept the offer. He took a calming breath. "Thank you. I'd appreciate the help if you think you'll still be safe. I'd never want to do anything to expose you." There. He sounded like their doctor again.

Beau squeezed his shoulder. "Don't worry. I'd never let anyone live long enough to take us down. But I'm glad to know you feel that strongly about our safety."

Austen nodded. He did care. Maybe he was upset, but he was strangely attached to them. "I should get home. Hopefully, Rain is still waiting."

A bright smile lit Kylo's face. "He texted me like five minutes ago saying his foot was elevated and he was thinking of ordering you two dinner."

Austen realized he smiled like an idiot. "That's good to know. For once, I'd really love not to ruin things because I always have to work."

Kylo linked arms with him and headed for the door. "Oh, you won't have to worry about that with Rain. If Rain understands nothing else, it's hard work. In fact, I'm surprised his strict regimen hasn't driven you insane yet. Rain doesn't rest. He was taught failure wasn't an option. In his world, failures die. He's honestly a bit intense. Rain has always acted like there's a knife at his throat when it comes to ballet. One missed step and it's over."

Austen felt like there were so many layers behind Kylo's words. Was there a knife to Rain's throat? They honestly didn't know that much about each other. Austen's attraction was so strong, it made him feel closer to Rain than they actually were. He needed to dig deeper. Austen would start tonight.

Warm lips brushed his nape and moved to the side of his neck. Rain drew a shaky breath as he reached over his shoulder and buried his fingers in Austen's hair. He should have startled and gone into fight mode at being pulled from his sleep. Instead, it was like he smelled Austen's cologne in his dreams and knew he was safe. He didn't have to fight.

"I brought you dinner."

"I know you did." Rain rolled, using the element of surprise to pin Austen beneath him. He took the kiss he wanted while going to work on Austen's jeans. The moment he had them torn open, Austen's dick was in his mouth. Rain skipped all spots in between. Austen kept getting away from him. Not this time.

Austen tolerated the blowjob for half a minute before Rain found himself on his back and blinking at the ceiling. He tore at Rain's clothes. "Sorry. I've wanted you for too long to blow in your mouth." He kissed Rain's stomach as he ripped off his pants. "I need to be inside you."

A loud moan dropped from his lips before Rain could stop it. Just the image of Austen fucking him was enough to have him on edge. He didn't recall being this obsessed and hot for anyone before Austen. In fact, Rain bordered on frigid. He didn't make space for others. Rain wanted Austen to take everything from him.

He watched through a haze of lust as Austen fought his way from his clothes. Austen had a condom and lube so fast, Rain didn't see where he got it. In his defense, the body Austen always kept hidden was beautiful. He had a chest Rain wanted to sleep on and arms he wanted holding him. The backs of Rain's eyes burned at the thought. No one held him. He wondered what that was like. Before he had time to fall down a rabbit hole inside his mind, Austen's slicked fingers stretched his asshole. Rain grabbed the headboard and held on. His hips left the mattress, seeking more. He was desperate.

Austen's crown pressed against his hole, and time froze. They held each other's stare as Austen slowly pressed inside. He was so pretty. The flush making his blue eyes pop had Rain twisted in knots. He looked turned on in a way that would sear into Rain's memory of the moment. In that second, Rain feared his heart. Not for what Austen could do to it, but for the way that stupid organ proved he was still weak, and for the all the ways he could break himself. Austen was good. No matter what he thought, Austen was pure. Rain was a weapon of controlled chaos and destruction. Then Austen thrust hard, and Rain forgot everything. All he knew was pleasure. Age definitely brought experience. Austen kept Rain held at the perfect angle as he pumped inside him. All Rain could do was cling to the headboard and get fucked. He was a mess. Rain had no idea how he looked because he couldn't do anything but fight his way toward the ecstasy Austen promised. He babbled and writhed. Whimpers and pleas tore from him. The experience was more than he could have dreamed. Austen kissed every place he could reach, biting and sucking as he took Rain. Rain wasn't an active participant. He was an instrument at the hands of a master. The pressure was right there, threatening what little sanity he possessed. Rain open-mouth fought for air as he strained toward release. Everything went silent. He held his breath. His muscles clenched and then an almost painful gasp ripped from him as he blew. His body jerked as cum jetted from his cock.

With his face pressed against Rain's shoulder, Austen's cries matched the rhythm of him taking Rain's ass. Rain realized his body moved with the sound, matching Austen. Dancing to the music they made. His muscles turned to gelatin when Austen's mouth covered his in a searching kiss. He heard the way Austen struggled to breathe, and pride filled him alongside the glow of satisfaction.

Austen's mouth moved to Rain's ear. He kissed its shell. "I really did bring you dinner."

A laugh burst from Rain. He was happy. For the first time, he was absolutely ecstatic, and Rain wouldn't let anything take this from him. Austen already knew he was crazy, but he didn't actually know a thing.

Chapter Five

AUSTEN STRETCHED LIKE A contented cat. A happy hum vibrated from the back of his throat. He couldn't stop. While straddling his ass, Rain painted designs on Austen's back in chocolate and then licked each one away.

"What's this?"

Austen focused on the brush strokes. "A star."

"Good boy." Rain licked, tracing the lines with this tongue and tormenting Austen.

A shaky breath escaped Austen as Rain moved lower. They hadn't left the bed all day. Austen had put down some towels, and they'd eaten in bed before the food had ended up on each other. It had been a long time since he felt this way. His muscles were completely relaxed. No stress touched his mind. Nothing existed outside of this bed.

Rain bit his ass cheek.

Austen moaned without meaning to.

He felt Rain smile against his skin. "That's a sensation you like, huh? You enjoy getting eaten?"

Austen pressed his face against the mattress. "Oh God." He didn't know how much more he could handle. While they had played all day and he wasn't as young as he used to be, Rain had him so fucking hard with all the licking and teasing. He would never smell chocolate again without getting an erection.

An evil chuckle vibrated against his ass. Rain shifted positions, moving to settle between his thighs. He felt chocolate dribble down his crack.

"Fuck." It was the breathless curse of a dying man.

Rain slapped his ass. "Lift those hips. Give me what I want."

Austen dutifully moved to his knees, giving Rain all the access he wanted. He held his breath and focused on every sensation. With that first swipe of Rain's tongue, moving toward his asshole, Austen nearly came. A sound he had never made fell from his lips. Thankfully, it was muffled by the mattress. He sounded exactly like a needy whore.

Rain didn't stop. His tongue explored every centimeter of Austen. He used the appendage against Austen in every way until Austen whined, begged, and rode his fingers and tongue with zero care of how desperate he looked. He was at a point of no return. If Rain stopped, he would die. Austen didn't think he was being dramatic at all. His life depended on Rain's tongue.

Rain moaned and Austen realized he stroked himself as he ate Austen. The thought alone was enough. His body jerked so hard, he felt a muscle tweak. The pain was gone as fast as it came, masked by the orgasm that shook his soul. Austen cried out against the mattress as he took what he wanted from

Rain's tongue. He had never come from this alone before. Rain hadn't once touched his dick. In a detached way, he heard Rain cry out, but all he knew was the pleasure dancing on his dick. He couldn't stop twitching out drops of cum. His muscles gave out while Rain kissed his spine.

A rhythmic buzzing cut through his joy. Austen thought he might cry. A whimper escaped him. Not now. His brain wouldn't work enough to help anyone. Rain had wrecked him.

"That's me, actually."

Austen couldn't move to even turn his head to watch Rain dig for his phone. Rain answered in Russian and stuck to that language. With his eyes closed, Austen enjoyed the cadence of each word. He was so tired. Sleep dragged on his soul.

Rain kissed his nape. "I'm sorry, beautiful. My family calls. You should sleep."

Austen pretended to cry. He didn't want to lose Rain. "No. Let's stay like this forever. Nobody needs to know where to find us."

Rain smiled against his skin. "I love this picture you paint. Unfortunately, I'm not free to make that choice."

It hit Austen. This was related to Rain's other job. The one they didn't talk about. He mentioned his family. Austen understood now why none of Rain's brothers looked like him. They weren't blood kin. They were killing kin. It was a brotherhood of assassins. That wasn't terrifying at all.

Austen rolled. Rain looked well satisfied, and Austen didn't want him to leave twice as badly. He ran his fingers through Rain's hair, trying to tame it from the mess they had made. "Please be careful. I'm pretty sure it would kill me if anything happened to you." Austen knew he sounded ridiculous. It was their first night together, except he had been so obsessed for so long, it didn't feel that way to him.

Rain turned his head and kissed the inside of Austen's wrist. His eyes closed as if he savored the moment. Austen couldn't look away. His heart twisted. He so desperately wanted this.

When Rain's beautiful eyes focused on him again, Austen stopped breathing. He saw his crazed infatuation mirrored back at him. "You never have to worry about me. I'll always come back to you."

Austen's throat swelled. This was really happening. They were doing this thing. "Okay. I'll always be waiting."

With a serious nod, sealing them as a them, Rain swiped a sweet kiss across Austen's lips. "Sleep."

As if Rain's demand cast a spell over him, Austen's eyes fell closed and wouldn't reopen. He felt Rain kiss his cheek and listened as he dressed. Austen was out before Rain was gone.

Flanked on all sides by his brothers, Rain kept his mind blank. He couldn't bring Austen here. Nothing beautiful belonged in his world. As they hit the mouth of the alleyway between two buildings owned by a key client of their Russian foes, they spread out, taking up their usual posts. Edge and Ridge scaled the buildings with ease, taking up sniper positions. As always, Shore and Field were already in position on ground sniper duty. Shadow did his job, moving in step with Rain and watching his back.

"Area clear." Tracker's voice came through his earpiece, letting Rain know he was good to go. With cameras already in place for days, Tracker would cover every inch they couldn't see.

Rain dipped low. His every step turned lighter, making no noise as a dance routine fired to life in his mind. Each move rehearsed, ensuring they all made it home alive. He didn't have to think about anything. Shadow had him covered. Rain could move exactly like that—like the rain... uncatchable. He could destroy everything in his path with deceptive ease. Tonight, he would do just that. He used his years of training and flexibility to slip inside the nondescript brick building, avoiding motion sensors with ease. As always, Shadow moved with him as if they were one. A lone light shone through an open doorway. Men's voices carried through the otherwise vacant building. They laughed. Smoke poured from the door. The sound of money quickly flitting through counting machines fought to be the loudest sound in the building. Rain kept his gaze locked on his target as he slipped knives from their sheaths. With one in each hand, he crept closer. Shadow was back-to-back with him, mimicking every move, and proving why they were so beautiful together on the stage. They were always in perfect unison.

Rain paused. He measured each breath as he readied his stance. The world held its breath. Nothing existed beyond the prey locked in his sights.

"Now."

At Tracker's order, he sprang. With Shadow keeping pace, blood sprayed through the air. They spun in unison. Men grabbed their throats, falling slowly to the floor one right after the other. Using Shadow's back as leverage, Rain ran up the wall, avoiding a lunge his way. Another throat gone. This time at Shadow's blade. Then everything went quiet. Only the sound of men choking on their blood filled the otherwise silent building.

"Clear."

In reverse, Rain and Shadow retraced their steps, avoiding carefully placed alarms. Their black clothes hid the blood that covered them, but the coppery scent still filled his nostrils. Tidy and Crisp would ensure all the mess disappeared, and the money was cleaned before finding its new home. At the mouth of the alleyway, Edge and Ridge scrambled from the buildings, flanking them. In ten steps, Shore and Field appeared. As a solid unit, they returned to the van. Another successful job complete.

Rain's mind immediately turned to Austen—alone and sleeping in a warm bed. Rain wanted to be there.

"Where were you all day?"

Edge's question was the first words spoken among the group since they left for the night.

Rain pulled a face with his LED mask. He was allowed a personal life. At least, he thought he was. Sometimes he wasn't so sure.

Edge snagged Rain's mask and pulled it off. "Use your words."

Rain sighed. He genuinely hated sharing this one thing. It was his and his alone. "I met with a surgeon about my foot. He's supposed to be the best in the country. So I made arrangements to have my surgery as soon as this run ends. He promised I'll be back on stage before the next run begins."

Edge lost the cold tone. His features softened. "Oh. That's good. I'm glad you're admitting this needs to be addressed. I know you're tough, but your refusal to treat your injury could be the thing that ruins your career."

A smile snapped to Rain's lips without a thought. "That's exactly what he said. I get it. It'll get fixed."

Edge nodded.

Rain nearly sighed when Edge focused on someone else.

"Text the client, Field." He touched his earpiece. "Send video proof, Tracker. Let me know when payment is confirmed."

Silence met his demands. They all waited, equally understanding nonpayment meant a second job tonight. It was just as well rehearsed, but they didn't want to do it. Getting paid was always best.

"Payment complete."

Even though no one sighed in relief, it was practically understood. Killing a client came with a lot more risks. They would know the crew came for them. That was the terms. Payment or death. A person who expected to die set up protection. That made things trickier. Rain could do it. No problem, but he still didn't like the extra complications. Plus, a sexy man waited for him. Rain needed to shower and then sneak out for the night. He wasn't exactly sure why he hid Austen. Rain just wasn't ready to introduce him. Killers Inc. was a brotherhood. They were family. His family would take it out of Austen, testing his mettle. Rain wasn't ready for that. He wasn't sure Austen would stay through that bullshit. Rain just needed a little more time. He could addict Austen to his touch. Then maybe they could survive his crazy brothers. Until then, it was his little secret. No one had to know.

Chapter Six

THE TWO WEEKS AUSTEN had to wait to do Rain's surgery were hell. He finally got to see Rain's performance from beginning to end. Austen spent the entire time wincing. While Rain never showed an ounce of weakness or missed a step, sometimes Austen saw the pain in his eyes when he thought Austen wasn't watching. He was so fucking grateful to have Rain on the table about to go under.

His medical staff and surgical crew readied the room while Austen sat near Rain's head. He waited for the anesthesiologist to run through everything with Rain before stealing his attention.

"Thank you."

Confusion crossed Rain's features. "For what?"

"Trusting me to take care of you."

Rain's features cleared. "Oh. That's nothing. I trust you above all others. There's no miracle you can't perform."

Austen realized he was smiling. Everything about Rain always fluffed his ego. "Thanks to Beau finding me some help, I've cleared my schedule for the next few weeks. Guess who's getting pampered?"

Rain chuckled as the anesthesiologist put an oxygen mask on him. Austen gave the guy a nod. He started the IV.

"I'll be the first thing you see when you wake up."

Rain nodded. His eyes were already drooping.

Austen kept an eye on his vitals. "Okay, guys. Let's get started."

Even though Austen went through the motions, he was hyper aware it was Rain. He went slowly, taking his time and ensuring everything was completely perfect before finishing up. Rain would stay off this foot until it healed if it was the last thing Austen did. He gave a few instructions to the team and then headed out to remove his PPE for sterilization. As he stepped from the room, muscular arms encircled him, lifting him from the floor. A sea of men wearing all black and various-colored LED masks surrounded him. Rage flared through Austen.

"I have a patient on the table. What in the fuck is wrong with you people?"

He went ignored.

The largest of the bunch motioned toward the room where Rain would wake soon. "Ridge. Shore. Clear the room. You know what to do. Shadow. Take care of your boy."

Three men broke off and headed inside the surgical suite. Gasps and screams filled the air, making Austen's already snapped temper skyrocket. "If you let Rain die, I swear to God you won't live to regret it." He struggled against the hold of whoever held him. It was like being trapped in a steel vise. "I have the connections to make you wish you were dead."

"Let's find a place to talk. You took my brother. I can't let that stand."

While he had thought this was likely the family Rain spoke of, realizing he was correct didn't make him feel better. They still endangered Rain with their bullshit. Not to mention terrorizing his staff.

"This isn't a kidnapping. It's foot surgery, dumbass."

Nobody moved, but the hold on him didn't lessen. An alarm sounded.

A guy with black hair and crystal blue eyes stuck his head out the door. "Um. Something's wrong."

The shot of panic that hit Austen gave him superhuman strength. With a solid elbow and head butt, he was free and back with Rain. He eyed the machines. Rain didn't have a heartbeat. "Get my fucking staff." Austen leaped onto the table and started CPR. Rain would not die on his watch, especially not because of his fucked-up family leaving him unsupervised within minutes of surgery. These motherfuckers. He would see them dead. Austen had never felt so much fury in his life. He had nowhere to go with it. His skills and the best team money could buy saved him. He worked, and they worked until they had Rain stable again.

"Pump him full of clot buster. When he wakes up, we'll start him on an anticoagulant." Austen pressed his forehead against Rain's and took a shaky breath. His entire body shook with fear and unchecked rage. No one had fought to be with him the way Rain had. No one meant as much to him. The more he thought about losing Rain, the more the fury built.

He needed to clean up and be ready for when Rain woke. Austen couldn't let the anger win. He had an amazing man counting on him. Austen turned. A group of mask-less, guilty-looking men stood behind him. Everything inside Austen exploded.

"What in the fuck were you thinking?" He tore off his gown. "He could've died." Austen screamed the words at the top of his lungs while motioning behind him. "Is that what you want? Is that what you were trying to do?"

The obvious leader of the bunch—like a dumbass—spoke up. "He disappeared without letting us know where he was."

"That's because he's a grown fucking man!" Austen couldn't stop shouting. "Let me tell you." He took a step forward, ready to fight them all. "The first goddamn thing you'll do is apologize to all these people you terrorized. I suggest you fucking mean it, or I'll make you disappear. You might think I'm weak, but I promise you I'm not. No one will ever find your bodies."

"Damn. I like him."

Austen ignored the smiling red-haired man who he had seen once at Rain's place. "Then, when Rain wakes up, not only will you confess what you've done, you'll beg his forgiveness. You better hope he gives it because you'll never have mine after almost stealing the other half of my heart."

"Austen." The weak-sounding voice had Austen spinning toward the table. Rain was awake. He looked groggy and confused. "Why are you yelling?" He swallowed. "My throat hurts."

Austen motioned for a nurse to get some water. He cradled Rain's head. "It's okay, baby. I've got some water coming."

"My chest hurts."

Fuck. He wasn't ready to explain that. Plus, he fully expected the dumbasses to do that.

He looked toward a different nurse.

She immediately pushed a needle of pain meds through the IV.

"That'll stop in a second." He kissed Rain's forehead. Tears filled his eyes. His anger showed its true face: terror. When he pulled away, Rain was out again. Austen straightened. He cleared his throat. "Thank you for the amazing job today. I appreciate you more than you know. Please keep me informed of any changes. I'll be back in a few minutes." Austen headed toward a different door, choosing to go a way that wouldn't force him to face the objects of his current hatred.

"Let's talk, Austen."

Austen held a finger up and kept walking. He couldn't do this right now. Austen had never been more frightened of himself. One wrong word and he might make good on his threats. Rain would never forgive that.

Rain slowly came awake. A set of crystal blue eyes stared down at him, startling the hell out of him. His heart rate jumped through the roof. A machine blared.

"Oh, good. You're awake."

"What's happened?" Austen's panicked voice broke through his confusion. He shoved Shadow aside to get to Rain. His gaze swept every machine, studying each one before focusing on Rain. He softened. "Hey, baby. How are you feeling?"

His gaze swept Austen's bedroom. Machines were parked next to one side of the bed, monitoring Rain's vitals. His brothers crammed the other side of the room. "Confused." He dragged the word out, unsure of why there was a crowd. Alarms clanged in his head when his entire family avoided his gaze.

Austen stroked his arm. "It's okay. A blood clot broke loose after surgery, stopping your heart. I had to do CPR, but you're good. As for the rest, I'll let your dumbass brothers explain."

Rain blinked at not only the hatred in Austen's voice, but the way his brothers allowed it. "Oh no." He didn't know what happened, but he knew it was bad. His family never looked guilty, and Austen never looked enraged. He sat up.

"You should rest."

Rain shook his head. "I'm fine." He really was. While he was sore, he felt more rested than he had in ages. Austen rushed around, fluffing pillows behind his back and using more to elevate his foot.

"I'm your shadow."

Rain took Shadow's hand. "I know that, sweetie." Shadow was his person. It had always been them. They had to be perfectly in sync. That took hours of work and unwavering trust. They had to know each other's minds like their own.

"You didn't give us an exact date for your surgery."

Edge's claim did nothing to clear his confusion. "Yes, I did. I told you it was immediately after the run ended."

"Some of us tried to say that," Shadow said, sounding condescending in a way they only spoke to each other.

After all the fussing over him, even en-suring a cup of ice water and a bottle of pills sat nearby, Austen climbed into bed with him on his other side and cuddled close.

Rain flashed him a smile. "I thought you said you'd be the first face I saw when I woke up."

Austen didn't smile. "Oh, they're not through."

Rain's gaze slid back toward the group of men who had each found chairs like they were part of an audience, and the show was watching Rain sleep. He knew them. They weren't their usual cocky selves. "What did you do?"

Edge cleared his throat. He crossed his legs at the ankles and uncrossed them again. "Like I said, we didn't have an exact date and you just kind of dropped off the map."

They were all in black—like dressed for a job. Suspicion and horror built. "And?"

"So we came to get you," Field finished for Edge.

Rain stared at the usually laughing red-haired jokester. "You didn't." He needed someone to say that hadn't stormed Austen's home.

"We tried to call. We even tried the work line. You've never ignored us."

At Edge's claim, Rain rubbed his forehead. "Why do I have a feeling this gets worse?"

"Because it does," Shadow said, sounding bitter. He knew Shadow would never willingly do something this stupid without protest, but Edge was the boss.

"Someone needs to spit it out. I'm in too much pain to pull fucking teeth today."

"Do you need some meds?" Austen was back to looking like the worried mother hen.

Rain kissed him. "I'm tougher than I look."

"Not suffering doesn't lessen your toughness. I know you're strong."

"We cleared the surgical room, and you were left without medical staff directly after surgery. That's when the blood clot broke loose and almost killed you. If we hadn't shown up here, you would've been monitored and kept safe." Shadow said the words fast, as if he couldn't take everyone else's silence and pussy-footing. After all, he was Rain's shadow. They were too much alike to endure nonsense.

Horror washed over Rain. His gaze moved from guilty face to guilty face. "Please tell me you're joking."

Field piped up. "For what it's worth, your man threatened to kill us and make sure no one ever found our bodies."

"As he should," Tracker added. "It's just as Edge said. We couldn't reach you and that's never happened. I tracked your phone here, and we worried you were being held against your will. We don't know your man. He could be anyone. That surgical room could've been prepared as an attempt to extract information. It's a home suite, after all. We didn't expect you to have surgery in some dude's house."

"He's not some dude," Rain said, hearing the exasperation in his voice. "Austen is the top surgical physician in the world. He treats only the most influential clients. They don't go to doctors' offices or hospitals. He goes to them or sees them here. Fucking Beau Bosi can't walk into County General with a bullet wound."

Nine heads bobbed in agreement, but Tracker continued to be their mouthpiece. "We know that now, but you should've said something sooner. You keep secrets." He motioned toward Austen. "If he's so special, why would you hide him?"

"Because he's special." Rain didn't look Austen's way as he made the confession. "I don't know how to force all this on him." He swept his arm wide their way. "Look at all of you. You don't know how to act." He focused on Shadow. "That doesn't include you, babe."

"I know." Shadow sounded as confident as he should. He would never condone this.

Edge shot Shadow a look as if he was a traitor.

Rain's temper made an appearance. "Don't look at him like that. You're the one who called for this bullshit plan. You almost killed me."

Edge's expression immediately shifted to guilty again. "I know. I'm sorry. It's my job to keep you all safe. If any of you go missing, it's my job to rescue you. What if someone had really taken you? Wouldn't you want us to come for you?"

Rain pinched the spot between his eyes. It wasn't that he didn't understand their side, but he was tired. So goddamn exhausted, and it had nothing to do with surgery or almost dying. For once, he wanted something normal. That was what Austen gave him. A normal life with pampering and love. No one else truly cared if his foot fell off dancing. They would blame him for not quitting ballet and toss his rotten foot in the trash.

Austen sat with his back against the headboard and tugged Rain into his arms. He kissed the top of Rain's head. "It's okay, baby. I'd never let anything happen to you. No matter how many idiots stood in my way."

A laugh burst from Rain at the bitterness in Austen's voice. It would be a long time before he forgave this one, and Rain couldn't blame him.

"I gave everyone on staff a hundred thousand apiece, if that helps," Edge said, cutting through Rain's annoyance.

A guy in scrubs came into the room. "Knock. Knock. Sorry. I need to take out your IV."

Rain nodded and held out his arm. He stared at the guy while he worked. "Were you here?"

A sweet smile flashed his way. "Yeah."

Rain's eyes fell closed. "I'm so sorry."

The guy winked. "Don't be. I'm happy to work with any doctor who brings down the roof for us the way Dr. Flowers did. The staff here have never felt safer or more appreciated."

Rain looked Austen's way.

He seemed almost embarrassed. "You flatlined. I might've shown out a little."

A few nervous chuckles rumbled around the room.

"It was awesome," Field said, returning to his ridiculous self. "I hope to have a fierce zaddy one day too."

Rain covered his eyes. They were really proving why he hadn't introduced them.

Austen chuckled.

The sound made Rain smile. He didn't know where this shit show was headed with his family, but he was glad he had Austen. Just like Austen's staff, he had never felt more protected. He hoped like hell he could keep him.

Chapter Seven

WHILE AUSTEN TREATED RAIN like an absolute dream, he felt like they tiptoed around the subject of his family. Rain knew Austen deserved answers. He knew Austen needed to fully know him if they were in this for the long haul. Rain just wasn't ready to expose another weakness. It was bad enough Austen already cared for him at his lowest.

But as Rain stared at Austen with nothing but the light from the TV highlighting his gorgeous body next to him in bed, he knew he couldn't hide. It was way too soon. They had only been dating for two months. Unfortunately, Rain couldn't pretend to need help any longer and he would need to get back to real life soon. If he hoped to hang on to this beautiful thing, he had to drag out the ugly for Austen to see.

"We were all raised together in a spy program in Russia."

Austen turned his head and focused on Rain. His eyes looked dark in the low light. That made it easier for Rain to keep going.

"My brothers and I," he clarified. Rain understood he had just started talking as if Austen could read his mind and knew what he never stopped worrying about. "It's a huge program. Ridiculously so. We were raised to infiltrate and blend in while having the skills of the deadliest soldiers." Rain swallowed. He hated his past, but it felt twice as ugly showing it to Austen. "I'm not even sure where we came from. Surely, we had parents or something, but all that was stripped from us, so I don't remember a time before them." Rain twisted his fingers. There was so much he would never say. Killers weren't born. They were forged by fire. He wouldn't expose someone beautiful like Austen to that.

He cleared his throat. "It's not safe to be gay in Russia. That goes double for the position we were in. There were many beautiful girls in the program when I really started to think of such things. In fact, we were chosen for our beauty. Pretty faces get access to more places." He knew he was stalling, dragging things out. Rain couldn't stop. His chest hurt. "I knew I was different when all my thoughts toward girls were nonexistent while so many of the others taunted them. Still, I tried incredibly hard to be straight. Pain came to those who didn't conform. Shadow found me first. We knew we were the same, but didn't say the words. Since we were so similar in size, we were paired to work with each other, honing our skills as a team. Having him saved my sanity."

Rain couldn't stop twisting his fingers. While he didn't think Austen would reject him, he didn't want to relive his past. "Shadow caught Ridge's eye. Too many times, their glances lasted too long. People started to notice. Before long, Edge and Tracker had joined our little group of outcasts. No one was openly friends, but we knew we had each other's backs. Then more found us. Field and Crisp. Tidy, Park, and Scout.

The list goes on. We ensured we made the perfect teams. Each named for our role. We all honed that skill to perfection, so no one split us apart. Unfortunately, the more of us that came together, the louder people talked. I don't know if it was jealousy or simply bigotry, but no one kept our secret."

For a moment, Rain rubbed his hands together. He couldn't make them warm or find his voice.

Austen set his hand over Rain's. "It's okay. You don't have to tell me. Just tell me this thing is a private company now and you're not still working for Russia."

Relief washed over Rain. A chuckle escaped him. "No. I'm definitely not working for them." He hesitated. "That doesn't mean I'm safe, though. In fact, that's why you need to know this. After weeks of torture, we rioted our way to freedom and escaped to America. We band together and work what we know. But the Russian government still wants us very much dead, and we never know when or how'll they'll strike. It's been silent for years, but I can't get complacent. It would kill me if anything happened to you."

Austen dragged Rain beneath him, covering him like a human blanket. He swiped a kiss so sweet across his lips, it made Rain's eyes burn. "There's no risk I wouldn't take to stay with you. Not to mention, every day I know one of my clients might decide I've seen too much. I've always lived with danger hanging over my head. I stay vigilant and strapped. You don't have to worry so much. I'm not going anywhere."

"Why?"

Austen—who had been trying to nuzzle Rain's neck—chuckled at the question. He lifted his head. His eyes shone bright with laughter. "What do you mean, why?"

Rain had never felt more serious. He needed this conversation. "Why do you want this? Why aren't you scared of who I am?"

The sweetest smile Rain had ever seen touched Austen's lips. "Because I love you. There's no way you don't know that."

Rain's throat swelled. The weight of Austen's confession fell on him. Austen loved him. Him. That was insane. Austen's other admission swept over his mind. It hadn't occurred to him how much danger Austen was in from just who his practice served. He would kill any of those old bastards who thought Austen had seen too much. Rain would see them all dead before he let a single hair on Austen's head get touched. This was his man. His heart. Austen deserved to know it. "I love you too. Tell me there's no way you don't know it."

Austen stole a kiss before answering. "I feel you every second of every day. You're meant to be mine. I can't explain that. In fact, I can't explain anything that's happened since I first set eyes on you." A dreamy expression overcame Austen's features. "You're just mine and I'm yours."

Rain could barely breathe. Every word Austen said was perfect and true. He couldn't lose this. Rain would do what–

ever it took. Kill whoever he had to. Austen would always be his. There was no escaping him now.

He couldn't believe Rain admitted to loving him. Austen had never felt so high. He had taken a colossal risk by saying the words first, but it was Rain. They were just comfortable and fit. It murdered his soul to know Rain's life had been so bad, but Austen had figured as much. He hadn't even asked because he didn't need Rain to dig into old wounds to get closer to him. Austen already felt closer to Rain than he ever had anyone.

His hand slid up Rain's bare torso as their tongues played. He adored every line of Rain's body. While Austen understood these past weeks of lounging around wasn't what their life would normally look like together, he had loved every second. He wished it could be like this forever. In reality, they had jobs they couldn't avoid forever. Rain wouldn't let Austen keep him tied between the bed and doing physical therapy. At least Austen knew he had given Rain the tools he needed to go back to the stage without being in constant pain. He provided for his man. Austen wanted to keep doing it.

Things turned heated. They hadn't made love since Rain's surgery. That was Austen's fault. He had almost lost Rain, and Austen needed to keep him safe. Rain had to be in perfect health again, or Austen just couldn't risk it. Unfortunately, his dick was beyond hard and had taken charge. He would stop if Rain wanted that, but Rain wasn't complaining and Austen needed him. He massaged Rain's cock through his thin pajama pants. Rain moved restlessly against his palm. Before he could stop himself, Austen had Rain's dick out and in his mouth. Everything about Rain made him hot as hell.

Rain tugged his hair. "Please? Oh, God. Please? I want to feel you stretching me wide."

That was all Austen needed to hear. He was on his feet, stripping and finding a condom. Rain scrambled from his clothes and lubed his asshole. They came together like it had been years since they touched. Rain bit Austen's bottom lip and held on as Austen thrust his way inside. The moment bordered on violence, except their fingers were linked and it felt like an act of love. That didn't mean he didn't have Rain folded up like a pretzel while he pillaged his ass. Austen had lost all hints of being gentle. He took Rain. Every sound Rain made proved he loved it. The way Rain blew within minutes also said a lot.

With his eyes squeezed closed, Austen savored every sensation. He burned the moment into his memory. Austen want-ed to remember every second they were together. The tension built and stole his focus. His thrusts got even harder as the coil tightened. A cry tore from him as he came unglued. It was like he flew. There was so much freedom in the experience. He felt accepted and loved in a way he never had. They were so fucking perfect for each other.

"I love you."

Austen's throat unexpectedly swelled at the sweetly whispered words against his shoulder. No one understood how badly he wanted to live like this forever. "I love you too." God help him. He wished he could stop there, but he was too in his feelings. "You have no idea how much I'd give to live like this forever. It's wrecking me, thinking about you not sleeping in my arms. You're supposed to be with me."

Rain kept lightly kissing his shoulder, but he didn't respond. Austen swore he wouldn't say the words again. He shouldn't have said anything to begin with. Admitting his love had already been insane enough for such a short time dating. He would stop there and be happy. That was what being an adult meant, accepting hard truths. Rain Agafonov would never fully be his. Austen had to be okay with that. No matter how much it sucked.

Chapter Eight

THE BIG, ADORABLE DUDE in combat boots toed the ground and smiled sweetly while Austen spoke to him. Edge couldn't hear what was said. Regretfully, he hadn't set up full surveillance yet on Austen's home. Rain hadn't stepped foot from it before today in the last six weeks and he knew Rain would bust him in seconds if he did anything. He could sit here, though. Edge could keep watch. It was a good thing he did. The moment Rain went to his rehearsal, another dude was on Austen's doorstep. Granted, Austen didn't invite him inside. He held the six-pack the guy had brought him and smiled as they talked. It was obvious they knew each other well. It was equally apparent the young one had a crush. His body language said it all. He kept tugging at his shoulder-length blond hair and shifting his feet. The guy was a mixture of nerves and happiness. Edge was enraged.

How much could Rain actually know about this doctor? While even Edge had to admit it was obvious the guy genuinely cared about Rain, what did he know? Like who was this guy that had waited until the exact day Rain left to show himself? Had he been watching the house, waiting for his shot? Maybe Austen had called him the moment Rain left to let him know the coast was clear. Austen still hadn't invited him inside and the more Edge thought about it, the more irritated he became by Austen's guest. His jaw ticked. He felt himself turning into the stalking predator he was. The moment Austen went inside, and the blond jogged down the steps, Edge was out of the van. He kept his gun and knife hidden as he slipped into position. The moment he could, he struck. With the gun's barrel at his nape and a knife at his kidney, he took control.

"Head for the van."

A low, deadly-sounding chuckle met his demand. "Oh boy, are you going to regret this."

Edge was too in his feelings. This guy was trying to take Rain's man. They weren't people who found happiness. Rain had. No one would take it from him. "I don't ask twice." Even Edge heard the truth to his words.

With a shrug that got under Edge's skin, he headed for the black van. Edge quickly secured him in the caged back before jumping behind the wheel. He double-checked to make sure no one played witness before pulling away from the curb. Eerie silence filled the back. Edge had to check the rearview mirror to make sure he still had a hostage. The most beautiful green eyes he had ever seen stared back at him. They swam with laughter. Edge had never been more fascinated.

"What's your name?"

"Why would I give you that?" The guy paused. "Better yet, why would you abduct a total stranger?"

"I'm Edge," Edge said, rather than answering.

"Well, that was dumb, Edge. Almost as idiotic as choosing me as your victim. We don't have to talk."

He sat back, stealing Edge's occasional glances into the mirror to see those eyes.

Truthfully, this was one of the dumbest things he had done in a long time. He didn't act unplanned. Edge didn't go off script. He was the script. Edge had no clue why this whole Rain and Austen thing was so under his skin. He didn't think he was jealous. Edge took a steadying breath. He was scared. Their team had always been their team. It felt like Rain slipped away, and what were they without each other? It wasn't a fate he had ever considered. They had sworn not to leave one another. Yet Rain was already as good as gone. This guy wouldn't steal that chance from

Rain. No matter Edge's feelings. Rain deserved a shot at real freedom. Edge just wasn't sure yet if he would let him have it. They were too vulnerable apart, especially Rain. Everything had always been about him. He was too beautiful. Rain had made high-ranking men feel things they didn't want. Not wanting those desires hadn't stopped them from acting on them. If not for that, they might not have ended up here, living together and thriving. Rain would get his happiness.

At the house, Edge chose the door they always went through when they had a visitor in tow. He knew Tracker would see them on the cameras and have the team gathered before they made it inside. They would find out who this guy was and why he had sought Austen with beer in hand and looking like a man on the hunt for a date. He slid open the back door, and the blond stepped out, completely calm to the point of cockiness. In fact, he seemed to find the entire experience amusing. Edge motioned toward the door with his gun. With a smirk, the guy headed inside. Just as Edge knew there would be, the team was armed and gathered. A chair already waited for interrogation. The guy sat like he had been here before.

Edge didn't bother explaining. He knew the team would roll with whatever. That was what they did.

He crossed his arms over his chest and eyed their visitor. "I ask again, what's your name?"

Nothing. Just a silent, smug stare.

Edge sighed dramatically. He motioned around the room. "Welcome to casa de Agafonov." It didn't matter what he admitted. Blondie likely wasn't leaving there. "As I've already said, I'm Edge." He waved Tracker's way. "The guy manning the cameras is Tracker." He started pointing at people. "Ridge, Field, Shadow, and Crisp. We're missing some people today, but I wasn't expecting company."

The guy's amazing eyes flickered to each person as they were named—like he took notes and made a list for later. He didn't speak. It was almost unnerving.

Edge opened his mouth, losing patience, and ready to notch things up. The door exploded inward. A huge guy with salt and pepper hair and cold brown eyes stormed into the room. With a gun in each hand, his gaze stayed on the move, watching for attacks.

"How in the fuck?" Tracker sounded baffled and horrified, proving the guy had somehow avoided their full security setup.

The new arrival tossed a look Blondie's way. "You good, Mickey?"

Mickey. Yum. The satisfaction that roared through Edge was almost orgasmic. He had a name.

"Yep." Mickey let the 'p' pop as if having the time of his life.

Field lunged. In a move so fast he didn't see how it happened, Field was on his back with the guy's heavy work boot on his throat. He didn't lose a gun or look winded.

"Go get in the car, Mickey."

Mickey popped from the chair. He tossed a wink Edge's way and strolled from the house. Edge's gaze never wavered from his confident swagger. Jesus. Edge's mouth was the Sahara. He wanted to give chase. Edge craved more of this insanity.

Field ran his hand up the leg connected to the foot on his throat. He let out an obnoxious-sounding moan. "Hurt me, Zaddy."

The new arrival didn't look amused. He took a step back. "This isn't a war you want. Beau Bosi sends his regards. He asked me to let you know, if you ever touch one of his again, he'll wipe this merry band of bitches off the face of the planet. He'll make the Russian government look like rent-a-cops."

That explained a lot. Edge dipped his chin. He recognized he was in the wrong. "Let Beau know it was a case of mistaken identity. Mickey is in no danger from us."

Field popped to his feet, smiling like the idiot he was. "You, on the other hand, you're welcome to come back and hurt me anytime."

The guy stuffed his guns in their hidden holsters. "Don't flatter yourself, kid. I'm a lot more than someone your age can handle."

The loud laugh that escaped Field made Edge smile. Damn, it had been one ridiculous morning. Not only did he have to explain his actions to his brothers, he had to beg them to keep this from Rain. Maybe one day he would stop acting crazy. Unfortunately, that day likely wouldn't come before he destroyed at least one relationship in this house. He chewed his bottom lip and watched Mickey's savior slip away. Edge had a name and a connection. He was willing to bet good money someone like Beau Bosi would make a good client, putting him one step closer to a new green-eyed obsession. Edge had to admit he was a sucker for green eyes. After all, that was truly what had him acting crazy now. But Rain had never been his and he never would be. It was time to let go.

Austen: *Mickey stopped by with a six-pack to apologize for pulling me away from you when he was sick.*

Rain: *Damn. That was like two months ago. Did he think you weren't over it?*

Austen: *Apparently, he was much worse than I realized. I was too irritated that day. He didn't get the care he deserved. One of the new physicians Beau found treated him, but he's been down for a while. It looked like he had lost a lot of weight. I feel bad.*

Rain: *Oh, baby. I'm sorry. It's my fault for keeping you from work. We'll find our balance.*

Austen: *I know. That doesn't mean I don't miss you like crazy, though.*

Rain: *Same.*

Rain squeezed his phone and stared at nothing. He was on his five-minute break between scenes. Ballet was ballet. He would learn his routine quickly. These performances had nothing on the steps he had to learn for his second career. Those were true dances. Beautiful art designed by Shadow and him. Rain leaned against the wall. Dancers stretched and twirled. Did he still love this place? Yes. Did he want another year-long run doing eight shows a week? No. As much as Rain hated to admit it, no. His gaze swept the room. When had he gotten so much older than everyone around him? He had survived this game way longer than dancers typically did. Honestly, Rain couldn't believe they still hired him for these parts. Before his surgery, he had fully believed he would keep at this until they tossed him from the building. After six weeks of being nonstop pampered by Austen, he didn't feel the same. There was something he loved more. Plus, it wasn't like Rain would never dance again. He found music in everything he did. Not to mention, he had Shadow. If he wanted, he could call Kylo. He didn't have to stop enjoying this thing he loved. Today, this didn't feel like love or joy. It felt like an exhausting chore standing in the way of those things. Austen wanted to hold him every night. Rain wanted that too. He just wasn't sure Austen was ready for what that might look like. Rain wasn't sure he could leave his brothers. They would all be more vulnerable. He didn't know what to do.

Music filled the air, signaling their return to rehearsal. Rain twisted his phone between his hands. It was now or never. If he stayed, Rain might never walk away. He loved this place too much. Rain needed advice. Yet he also knew he needed to make this decision alone or he would have someone to blame if he regretted it. Goddamn it.

Rain: *Are you home? I need to talk to you.*

Edge: *Yeah. You know I'm always here for you.*

He knew. That was why Rain couldn't leave his family, but he had heard the longing and fear when Austen admitted to never wanting to sleep apart. Austen would never bring it up again. Rain already knew that. That was who Austen was. He would never complain or guilt Rain. Austen would simply accept whatever scraps Rain gave him. Rain wanted Austen to have everything.

He had said this was real, and he meant it. Now was the time to prove it.

Without saying a word or looking back, Rain grabbed his bag and headed for the door. He almost made his escape.

Shadow appeared at his side and linked arms with him. "So it's over, huh?"

Horror raced through Rain. "No. You don't have to go with me. You still have all the years of dance you want left in you."

A sweet smile flashed Rain's way. "No, I don't. I've only stayed because you do. It's always been us with you leading the way. Honestly, I'm ready to go home."

It had never occurred to Rain that Shadow stayed on stage for him. Shadow was two years younger than him, but that was still old as far as dancers went.

It seemed he had been selfish. That ended tonight.

"My feet hurt."

A loud bark of laughter burst from Shadow at Rain's admission. "Mine too."

They shared a smile. It was time to go home. Rain had a feeling it was long overdue.

The house felt empty as hell without Rain. Austen had made a few house calls. He had paced the floor. His mind never stopped stewing over what Rain did at every given moment. Likely, he worked himself to death. He overdid it like he hadn't been down for six weeks. Austen felt that in his spirit. There was nothing he could do, though. That was just Rain, and Austen loved him exactly as he was.

The phone Austen held like a lifeline finally buzzed. Austen raced to open his messages. He smiled at the sight of Rain's name. Relief poured through him. Maybe it was foolish, but a small part of him half expected to never hear from Rain again. If that happened, he knew Rain would be out of his reach with his brothers looking out for him. That wouldn't stop Austen. He would just likely end up dead. It was possible Austen shouldn't have mentioned Rain staying in his bed every night from now on. Admittedly, he had danced around saying the actual words that he wanted them living together. Still, Rain wasn't dumb, but he might have run scared. That had been a genuine fear the entire day.

Rain: *If you're bored and/or not too busy, you should come to the dance studio.*

Austen didn't need to be told twice. He was on his feet in an instant, grabbing his keys and finding his shoes. The drive to where Rain's small private dance studio was on the other side of town felt like it took forever. He didn't even realize he had forgotten to turn on the radio until he pulled into the parking lot. Only a black van sat outside. Austen tried not to race to the door like an over eager idiot. It was hard, but he measured his pace. He was more than a little grateful when the door easily opened. Austen resented anything between him and Rain. His steps slowed the moment he stepped inside.

In the middle of the dance floor, back-to-back, Rain was in all white while Shadow wore all black. They each wore virtual reality glasses. Austen couldn't look away. They moved perfectly in sync. Whatever Rain did, Shadow did in reverse. It looked as if Rain ducked, slipping beneath whatever he saw inside his glasses. Shadow bent over backwards, staying perfectly glued and mimicking every move. They were amazing. He was enthralled. The talent they possessed was unlike anything he had ever seen. Whereas Rain was blond and light in every way, Shadow was dark. They were the same size. Almost identical. They each used the other's back for balance and strength. It also helped to keep time with each other and maneuver their virtual world. He didn't want to look away, but he couldn't ignore the rest of the room.

Tracker sat behind a laptop, giving the occasional order. He looked up and saw Austen. Tracker gave him a quick smile before going back to staring at the screen. Pairs of the brothers sat around the perimeter with their heads together, going over what looked to be schematics.

Edge appeared at his side with his own set of plans. "Hey there. Feel free to speak. You won't bother them. They're wearing noise-canceling earpieces. All they hear is Tracker."

Austen shook his head. He couldn't look away from the pair on the dance floor. "They can't even hear each other?"

Edge's dark gaze stayed locked on the papers he held. "They don't need to. They can feel each other. Now, Rain tells me you two briefly discussed living together." That brought Austen's head whipping around. Edge still didn't look his way. "It's not safe for Rain to leave the family." Edge finally focused on him. "He would. Rain would leave us for you. But I'm asking you to consider an alternative."

Austen was so blown away, he didn't know what to say or how to react. He couldn't believe Rain had told Edge they talked about moving in together. They hadn't, but that was what Austen wanted. It was obvious Rain didn't intend to ignore Austen's hints.

Edge kept talking like Austen wasn't reeling. "Obviously, we can't have patients showing up at our house. That's a security nightmare. However, we have a few supply buildings." He moved even closer and showed Austen the paper he held. "This one is the closest and easiest to convert to an office slash surgical facility. We could have it finished in no time, if you'd be willing to live with us instead. Let us keep Rain safe. You safe. He loves you. That's a weakness that can be exploited. Just think about it."

Austen had nothing. He had never considered leaving his home behind to live in a compound with a bunch of professional assassins. Hearing Edge say Rain loved him was hard to see past. He couldn't think of anything else. Not only had Rain admitted to loving him, but he had told his family too. It was humbling in a way he had never experienced. These people were dangerous.

His gaze slid toward the dance floor. In perfect harmony, a knife appeared in both hands of each man. They spun in flawless time, taking down invisible targets. It was the first time he had seen Rain as the killer he was. He didn't know what it said about him that he thought that shit was sexy as hell. Definitely nothing good, he was sure. That didn't stop him from seriously considering Edge's suggestion. He didn't know if he could give up the quiet privacy he enjoyed now. His gaze followed Rain's every move. He didn't know what to do, but he knew he couldn't lose Rain. No matter what it took.

Chapter Nine

WATER SLOSHED OVER THE edge of the tub as Rain scooted closer, making him glad they'd had the forethought to put down some towels. His tongue played with Austen's. The hot bubbly water surrounded them, easing Rain's tired muscles even as his body burned for Austen to take him. His heart begged to get closer. He could never get close enough. Rain tilted his head back as Austen sucked and bit his neck. He was in his version of heaven.

"I need to tell you something." Rain dug his fingertips into Austen's shoulders as he gasped out the words.

"Mhmm?" Austen licked his chin.

"I quit the ballet tonight."

Austen froze. He leaned away and met Rain's gaze. "Okay. Why? You love ballet."

A flush rode high on Austen's cheeks and his lips were swollen from their kisses. There was no missing how hard Austen was for him. Yet Austen obviously cared more about Rain's happiness than his body.

Rain's eyes burned. His nose stung. Every moment he spent with Austen proved he had made the right choice. "I love you more."

A deep line appeared between Austen's eyebrows. "I would never ask you to give up something you love for me."

Rain nodded. "You're amazing. I know you wouldn't. But the thought of spending the next year doing eight performances a week while I could be like this instead is too much for me." Rain took a breath. "And I'm tired, baby. Everything hurts. Today, I was standing there, and I realized I don't want it anymore. Not like I used to. Don't get me wrong, I'll never stop loving dancing. But the exhausting performances and dancing through the pain, I don't want that anymore. I want to be like this with you."

Austen leaned his head back against the rim of the deep tub and held Rain's stare. His closed expression gave nothing away. "There's nothing I crave more than to live my life like this, but I need to know you're happy. If you miss it or change your mind, then go back. I need to know you feel fulfilled."

A smile tugged at Rain's lips. He rocked forward, teasing himself. "I'd like to be filled, please."

Austen's expression never wavered from serious. "Let the water out."

Rain didn't hesitate to flip the lever, releasing the water from the tub.

Austen pointed at their waiting towels. "Dry off. I want to watch."

While Austen sat in a draining tub, Rain stepped out and did as told. He moved slowly, giving Austen the show he wanted. The way Austen's heated gaze stayed locked on him had Rain nearly panting. He had never felt so desired.

Finally, Austen stood. He climbed from the tub and took Rain's waist. Instead of pulling him close, the way Rain expected, Austen spun him to face the bathroom mirror. He urged Rain to lean over and hang on to the vanity.

"I want you to see what I do when I make love to you."

"Oh, God." He wouldn't make it.

Austen yanked open a drawer and pulled out an unopened bottle of lube.

Rain nearly danced in place in his impatience as he watched Austen take his sweet-ass time opening the bottle. When Austen finally fingered him, the neediest of sounds escaped him. He bit his lip, trying to stifle it. Then the way Austen watched his every reaction in the mirror had Rain letting go. Before that moment, he hadn't realized how much Austen got off on Rain's pleasure. That was sexy. Not every man cared, much less wanted their partner's happiness. Austen more than cared. It was part of the experience for him.

"You're looking at me. You're supposed to be looking at yourself." Austen impaled him.

Rain's gaze jumped to his reflection. He nearly blew. The pure and massive lust written all over him was way more than Rain expected. He knew how Austen made him feel, but he had never realized how much he couldn't hide it. Rain had been trained to hide his true emotions and only show whatever part he played. He was a real person with Austen. More than that. He was raw. Rain was clay and Austen shaped him.

Once he noticed, Rain couldn't tear his gaze away from his reflection as Austen fucked him. That was what it was too. This wasn't one of those slow love-makings that lasted all night. Austen took him. He already knew how Austen looked. Austen was always open in his hunger and pleasure. It was himself he didn't know. He was the stranger.

Rain knew Austen wanted him to see how needy he looked when they fucked. But Rain saw everything laid bare. He had become someone new since falling for Austen. Rain was the best and truest version of himself. He wanted to be better and normal. Rain wanted to be whoever stared back at him now. This guy only knew love. Tears filled Rain's eyes. It happened from nowhere. He maybe shouldn't have looked quite so closely.

Rain wasn't someone Austen should be proud to be with.

The world flipped, and he found himself in Austen's arms. Austen carried him to bed. He didn't say a word until Rain was beneath him, getting that slow lovemaking he had come to crave from Austen. Austen kissed away his tears.

"I love you."

"You shouldn't." Even as Austen made his body scream with pleasure, Rain couldn't stop trying to warn him. "You deserve so much better than this. I'll never be free or good."

Austen claimed his lips and kissed him deeply before responding. "Stop. I didn't go into this blind. From the first time we met, I knew you'd be mine. I felt in my soul you were my other half. Call me crazy. I knew. Please don't regret me now."

It hit Rain. Austen thought Rain doubted what they had. Rain grabbed his face and held it between his hands where Austen couldn't look away. "I love you. You are the other half of me. I don't think you're crazy because I felt the same." His throat swelled, and it sounded in his voice. "I'm scared as hell you'll see the real me and stop loving me. That would kill me."

Austen slowly lowered his head. He gently rocked inside Rain, hitting at the perfect angle. "Never."

Rain felt the vow in his soul. This was truly forever. Austen dug his hand beneath Rain and held Rain in place. Their kiss turned desperate as Austen's thrusts became almost violent. Rain clung to Austen and took it. His every fear and worry scattered. Austen would never let him hurt. He would never fail him. Austen truly loved him—warts and all. The tension coiled inside him, stealing his breath. He tore at Austen's skin, needing release. Then the world flew apart and Rain saw their future. He would spend the rest of his life shaking just like this. Rain wasn't disappointed.

In the back of his mind, even as he slept, Austen was always aware of Rain's body against his during the night. He always woke a little any time Rain left the bed, but he was always out again the second Rain was back. That was exactly why the spot turning cold beside him had his eyes shooting open. Unfortunately, it only happened a half second before he was ripped from the bed, making him slow on the uptake. His gaze shot around the room as his heart shot to his throat. Men in all black and LED masks scattered the room. One already had Rain on his feet and a knife to his throat.

As quickly as the panic hit, it died. His earlier conversation with Edge came back to haunt him. He was fucking pissed. These guys were such idiots. They couldn't give Austen one night to think about their offer. Of course, they would try to scare him into complying. That was who they were—dumbasses.

Austen had already decided. Rain had given up ballet for more time with him. Austen could give up a house.

The pure manipulation had Austen's temper shooting through the roof. No one could get him angry like Rain's family. "You've got to be fucking kidding me. What in the hell is wrong with you people?"

"Austen." Rain said his name so quietly and calmly that everything inside Austen stilled. He focused on Rain. Rain looked like a different person. Cold. Empty. It hit Austen. This was real. These weren't Rain's brothers. Austen held his stare. "Close your eyes. Don't look. Okay?"

The guy holding Rain jerked him closer, nicking his throat with the blade. He said something in Russian that sounded deadly to Austen without him even knowing the language.

Austen held Rain's stare for a second longer. He knew he looked at the killer Rain feared so much Austen would hate. Never. Austen closed his eyes.

Loud but quickly muted shouts followed by gurgling noises surrounded him. He was tugged harder from behind, but no pain came, and the knife was no longer pressed against his throat. Something warm splashed his skin. Time ticked by and silence fell. The temptation to open his eyes was massive as the scent of copper filled his nostrils.

"Keep your eyes closed."

Relief poured through him at the sound of Rain's voice. He hadn't realized how terrified he had been for Rain until he heard him.

Rain took his hand. "Follow my lead, but don't look."

"Okay." He was a doctor. A surgeon. He knew the scent of blood and had seen a lot of gruesome things. Austen understood that wasn't what Rain didn't want him to see. He didn't want Austen to get a look at the side of himself he hated and couldn't escape. Rain wanted this one part of his life untouched. Austen would give him that. Not only was Austen too blindly in love to care, Rain had just saved him. If he had been with anyone else, Austen would be dead. He didn't doubt that for a second.

Austen followed Rain's lead. He heard the shower start. Rain pushed him inside. Warm water poured over him.

"Count to twenty, and then you can open your eyes. I'll be back in a few."

Austen stood still and slowly counted inside his head. When he opened his eyes, he watched Rain drag a wet towel across the bathroom floor with his foot. Walking backward, he cleaned up a trail of blood. Austen turned away and worked to get clean. There was a bottle of hospital-strength sterilizing soap in his shower for just this reason. More than once, he had come home from work covered in blood. He wasn't always prepared for the destruction his clients called him in to repair. Austen took his time. He was glad he did when Rain climbed into the shower with him. He didn't have any blood on him. Austen assumed he cleaned up elsewhere before coming in for a final scrub. He didn't

say a word or look at Austen as Austen
used the same soap to wash him.

"I spoke with Edge at the dance studio
earlier. He showed me plans he's made
to turn one of the supply buildings into
a surgical center for me."

Rain finally met his stare. He looked
exactly like a man who expected to lose
everything now. "They'll be here soon to
clean up the mess. You won't have to
worry about any of this coming back to
you."

Austen kept going, talking over him.
"That way, I can move in with you and
not have to worry about things like
this."

"I'm sorry. You—"

Austen didn't stop speaking over him.
"If it means I get to hold you every night

for the rest of my life, then I'm good with that."

Rain held his stare. "I can keep us safe."

Austen nodded. "I never once doubted you." In fact, Austen had never been more impressed with anyone. Rain had taken out four men by himself and hadn't even been winded afterward. That wasn't the point. "Do you really want to sleep with one eye open forever? I know I don't want that for you. You have an adorable snore I'd miss."

Rain snorted. He slowly came back to life. "I don't snore."

"You absolutely do." He kissed the tip of Rain's nose. "It's a soft, cute snore."

Rain shook his head. "You're just making things up now. All you had to do was say you wanted to move in together. That's what I want too." He shifted from foot to foot. "If you still want me, that is."

Austen shuffled Rain against the wall. "Are you being serious?" Even Austen heard the hope in his voice. He ignored Rain's insecurity. Rain would be over that soon. "Are you really willing to live together?"

Rain held his stare. "I want this. I want us. Forever."

He knew Rain had said as much in the past, but this was different. They agreed to mix their lives and make them one. That was huge. It was life changing. He was fully aware he was older, and Rain should choose someone else. Austen was too selfish to point that out, though.

"Okay. Good." He tried to sound like an adult making an adult decision instead of showing the way he wanted to jump and cheer. His lips skimmed Rain's. A smile exploded across his face before he could stop it. "You're really mine. I can't believe it."

Rain deepened their kiss, as if he needed to taste Austen's happiness. Austen vowed, no matter what waited in the other room, nothing would spoil this moment. He just hoped Rain's brothers didn't make him regret this decision. That was his only true fear.

Chapter Ten

MANY TIMES OVER THE years, Rain had forgotten what it was like to love dancing. Every time, Kylo had given that back to him. He twirled around the kitchen with Kylo until they were both too dizzy to stand and laughing too hard to breathe. Then he threw Kylo a tea party. While Rain didn't have any Little tendencies, he didn't judge anyone who did, and it was nice enjoying something simplistic. Plus, the entire setup of tiny teacups and cookies made Kylo smile, and that meant everything to him.

"Is Austen completely moved in yet? I figured he must be, since Daddy said we can play whenever he does his blood pressure thing every three months. Austen used to come to us, but Daddy feels guilty for taking too much of his time away from you."

Rain smiled and hung on every word. In Beau's care, Kylo thrived. He was fully himself at all times, dressed like a schoolgirl and beaming with happiness. Rain might think it odd, considering he loved one of the most dangerous men alive, but so too did Austen. Since Rain knew the terrible things he would do to keep Austen safe and happy, he assumed Beau was the same for Kylo. Even killers loved something.

"Yeah. It's been a slow process since we needed to convert one of our supply buildings into a surgical center. Austen is still seeing most patients at his house until the new place is finished. Of course, you'll always be welcome here." Rain bit his bottom lip. He knew he could talk to Kylo about anything. Always had. Sometimes Rain hated his thoughts. "I feel guilty."

Kylo's sweet blue eyes looked so untainted by life as he stared at Rain, giving his full attention. "Why?" He picked up a cookie and nibbled it like a rat while he waited for Rain to respond.

Rain shook his head and fought a smile. God, the precious innocence. He knew exactly what Beau saw in Kylo. Kylo was probably the purest air he had ever breathed. "I'm not sure Austen wanted this. Don't get me wrong, I know he's happy to move in together. But I think he had a very different picture in mind for our future. Not giving up everything to live with a gaggle of idiots." Rain glanced over to tell Edge no offense, but the guy stared so intently at Kylo's personal guard, Mickey, that Rain doubted he had heard. In fact, Rain didn't even know why he hung out in the kitchen with them. Kylo wasn't his friend. He just sat at the table as if he couldn't trust Kylo or Mickey, which was dumb.

Rain shook his head and focused on Kylo again. "Someone broke into his home and tried to kill us. That forced his hand. I know he didn't want this." The more Rain talked, the surer he became. This wasn't the life he would have chosen for them.

Kylo made a dismissive gesture. "Austen and I are a lot alike. We both spent our lives alone. Just like he lived alone before you, I lived completely alone before Beau. Now I live in a house full of guards. They're not idiots, though. Maybe that's the difference?" Kylo shook his head and waved his arms, as if wiping away his entire speech. "Anyhow, I won't lie and say it didn't take time to get used to someone being around every corner, but—for me—it's nice. I hated the emptiness. Austen does too. We talked about it once. His career has isolated him in a lot of ways. Plus, he loves you way more than any amount of privacy."

"Not to mention you have your own space. It's not like he can't get away from us."

At Edge's interjection, Mickey shot him an irritated look. "You should stay out of it. If Austen ends up having a problem living here, it'll be because you're obviously an overbearing person. It's my job to be here. You're choosing nosiness."

Rain looked between them.

Kylo gnawed another cookie, looking unbothered.

Something wasn't right. As far as he knew, the pair had never met before today. Yet Mickey already had Edge pegged. Granted, he felt responsible for them and that was why he was so overprotective, but Mickey shouldn't be so sure in the opinion.

Rain motioned between them. "What's going on here?"

Kylo kicked his feet like a kid whose feet wouldn't touch the floor. "Mickey is still upset over Edge kidnapping him." He focused on Edge. "I'm not really happy about it either. He's my favorite."

A blinding smile exploded across Mickey's face.

Rain was confused as fuck.

Edge looked incredibly uncomfortable. "I'm pretty sure I apologized." The grumbled words had a hint of horror creeping through Rain.

"What did you do?"

Everyone ignored Rain's horrified-sounding question.

Mickey was focused on Edge with laughing eyes, but Rain saw the danger hidden beneath. He recognized why Beau had chosen him for Kylo. Mickey would do terrible things for Kylo, but he still had love in him. Rain wondered if they were about to get a good look at his bad side. "I'm certain you didn't. Maybe you apologized to Beau, but you didn't say it to me."

Edge held his stare. He looked at Mickey in a way Rain had only seen him look at one other person before. "I'm sorry."

"Not even making excuses, huh?"

Rain couldn't look away from the exchange.

"No excuses. I'm sorry."

Mickey nodded. "Fair enough." He poured more tea into Kylo's tiny teacup.

Edge never stopped watching his every move.

Rain forgot to ask why in the hell Edge had kidnapped Mickey or when any of this happened. His throat swelled. He genuinely hoped Edge didn't get hurt.

Edge's sanity wouldn't survive that kind of blow. Hatred of love was all Edge knew.

"Anyhow, my point was, you make Austen happy," Kylo said, acting as if Mickey and Edge's exchange never happened. "That outweighs everything else. And honestly, it's not like you could truly live alone. It's like Beau and me. He's too big of a target. You are too. You might as well live with people you love instead of strangers you've hired." He flashed Mickey a smile. "I couldn't imagine my life without our boys."

Despite everything, Rain smiled at Mickey getting called a boy. They were probably close to being the same age. His humor over the situation died as quickly as it hit. Austen wasn't Kylo, and Rain's family weren't Kylo's guards.

His family had done nothing to ingra-
tiate themselves. Austen would likely
be done with him in less than three
months.

Austen appeared with Shadow at his
side. They were laughing loudly as they
appeared in the doorway. Henry and
Beau were right behind them. Beau
didn't stand a chance of reaching his
husband first. Shadow spotted Kylo and
squealed like a child before launching
himself in Kylo's direction. The three
of them had been in several performances together. Everyone loved Kylo.
Rain watched them hug and talk ani-
matedly. He looked Beau's way, checking
for any signs of jealousy. Beau merely
looked like an indulgent father. Henry
leaned his shoulder against the door-
frame and stood watch. Rain's gaze slid
to Austen when Austen didn't imme-

diately come to him. He had stopped and spoke with Mickey. They smiled like they were good friends. That was not what caught and held his attention, though. Rain had been so focused on his thoughts and Shadow's reaction to seeing Kylo. He hadn't noticed Field being dragged along on Austen's leg—like a little kid, begging for attention. Austen stood at Edge's back with his hands resting on Edge's shoulders. Occasionally, he squeezed. Each time he did, Edge smiled even as he never looked away from Mickey. Austen was older than everyone in their family. He was like the loving father they'd never had.

Austen sighed loudly, snapping Rain from his trance of studying every detail. "For fuck's sake. It's in our bedroom. Go get what you want, and I'll pick some more up later."

Field popped from the floor. "Yes! You're the best." He kissed Austen's cheek and was out of the room like a shot. Austen pinched the spot between his eyes, but his smile spoke volumes. He was happy here. Kylo was right. Austen's life had been lonely. Rain had everything to offer him.

Austen dropped his hand and focused on Rain. "We'll have to go on a road trip later to grab some more of that organic peanut butter from that little local business two towns over."

"Get two jars," Field said around a spoon as he strolled into the kitchen. He had Austen's peanut butter jar clutched to his chest like it was gold.

Henry snorted.

Field shot him a flirtatious smile. "What? Are you jealous of my spoon?"

Austen shook his head. His gaze never wavered from Rain. "I might have to buy that goddamn organic store with the way Field eats."

"Can we, Daddy?"

Rain bit his bottom lip at Field's question. Austen looked like a man in love with his life.

Kylo linked fingers with Rain beneath the table and squeezed. His eyes stung as it hit him how beautiful his life was now. He one hundred percent didn't deserve it. Rain would take it nonetheless.

Austen stocked the cabinets in the small kitchen inside their bedroom. They had bought more things during their shopping trip than Austen intended. Luckily, more than half of it had been for the boys. Their personal kitchen cabinets weren't that big. It was still oddly nice, though. Austen felt like they had their own tiny apartment where Rain couldn't hide. He had to stay under Austen's feet. Austen loved having Rain beneath him.

"If you keep spoiling Field, he might chain himself to your leg. He's clingy like that."

Austen laughed at the image Rain painted. "Meh. I get the feeling no one has ever spoiled these boys. A little won't hurt."

Rain's arms encircled him. He pressed his lips against the spot between Austen's shoulder blades. Austen froze and savored the moment.

"It's so sexy when you act all daddy-like."

Austen couldn't stop smiling. He hadn't known so much happiness existed before Rain. His joy spread to everything, even the dumbasses he never expected to forgive. They were all young and only had each other. He had spent a lot of time with Edge, building the surgical center. The insight into their lives was eye-opening as they had grown closer. Austen understood now why they acted rashly when it came to their little chosen family. That was all any of them had to lose. Austen enjoyed showing them kindness. It was obvious they needed an adultier adult in their lives to curb their recklessness. It was also more than that.

"Maybe my motives are selfish. I've had no one to spoil over the years." He shrugged. "Truthfully, before you and with my parents gone, I've had no one period. It's been nice having a family."

Rain's hold tightened. "They love you."

A lump formed in Austen's throat unexpectedly. It was odd to go from an empty life and home to constantly surrounded. "I love you." They had only been together six months, but half a year felt like half a lifetime to Austen. That's how certain he was that he had found his place. His home. He never wanted to be anywhere else.

Rain stuck his arms beneath Austen's shirt—like he needed to be skin on skin. "I'd do a lot of crazy shit to keep you."

"Same." Even Austen heard how breathless he sounded. He loved every second of being held by Rain.

"That night you caught me in your bedroom wasn't the first night I broke in to watch you sleep."

A bark of surprised laughter burst from Austen. Every day, Rain made him realize how insane they were because he loved everything about this crazy ride. "That's okay. I used to sit and watch the theater so I could see you go inside for every performance. It was only a few seconds of watching you when you thought no one looked, but I lived for those moments."

He felt Rain smile against his spine. "I knew you were there."

Austen spun. "Are you joking?"

Rain's gorgeous smile spoke volumes. He was serious. "Do you honestly think it took me that long to get out of my car and to the door every single night?"

Austen shrugged. "You always had a lot of shit to carry in." Austen hesitated. In the end, he no longer cared how he looked. "I thought several times about using that as an excuse to talk to you. All I had to do was pretend to see you unexpectedly and then offer to help." Austen shook his head, laughing at his own ridiculousness. "You really make me act ways I never have before, and I have zero regrets."

"We should get married."

Austen had never been taken off guard so quickly. His brain suffered a rapid secession of misfires. And still he responded so fast, Rain had barely finished saying the words. "Yes. We should."

They stared at each other. Time ticked by with no meaning. It was as if they equally savored the miracle they had received in each other.

Finally, a smile exploded across Rain's face. "I should've asked in some crazy way that would have you questioning your sanity about saying yes."

Austen shrugged. "You still could. I'd still say yes."

Rain drew him down for a kiss. His lips swiped Austen's. "Best I save a little madness for after we're married. I'd hate to become tiresome."

"Married? You two are getting married? Hey, Rain and Austen are getting married!" Field shouted the words down the stairs. "We get to keep Daddy."

A stampede of boots sounded on the steps.

Austen chuckled against Rain's lips. "We have to get a better lock for that door."

Rain smiled, still trying to steal kisses. "It wouldn't matter. There's no lock they can't pick."

Austen pressed his forehead against Rain's and stared into the eyes of the man he loved. They stole a moment of silent celebration between them before the brat brigade crashed their way into the room. Austen understood his life would always be this way now. He had traded peace for this craziness. Austen had also traded the emptiest of quiet and bottomless loneliness. In return, he got the most blindingly beautiful love he had ever seen and a houseful of happiness. He definitely came out the winner in this deal.

Keep your eye out for the next Killers Inc., *Edge.*

About the Author

CHARITY PARKERSON IS AN award-winning and multi-published author with several companies. Born with no filter from her brain to her mouth, she decided to take this odd quirk and insert it in her characters. One of her greatest loves is writing morally gray characters. You'll find them scattered throughout her hundreds of titles.

*Nine-time Readers' Favorite Award Winner

*2015 Passionate Plume Award Finalist

*2013 Reviewers' Choice Award Winner

*2012 ARRA Finalist for Favorite Paranormal Romance

*Five-time winner of The Mistress of the Darkpath

Connect with her online:

*Sign up for her newsletter: https://bit.ly/charityparkersonnewsletter

*Join her readers' group on Facebook: http://bit.ly/CharitysTribe

*Website: https://www.charityparkerson.com

*A list of her social media accounts and giveaways all in one place: http://hy.page/charityparkerson